You Will Forever be my Always

A Novel

DAN McCRORY

Copyright © 2023 by Dan McCrory

ISBN: 978-1-77883-162-1 (Paperback)

All rights reserved. No part of this publication may be reproduced, distributed, or transmitted in any form or by any means, including photocopying, recording, or other electronic or mechanical methods, without the prior written permission of the publisher, except in the case brief quotations embodied in critical reviews and other noncommercial uses permitted by copyright law.

The views expressed in this book are solely those of the author and do not necessarily reflect the views of the publisher, and the publisher hereby disclaims any responsibility for them.

BookSide Press
877-741-8091
www.booksidepress.com
orders@booksidepress.com

Contents

Chapter 1 1
Chapter 2 5
Chapter 3 9
Chapter 4 11
Chapter 5 12
Chapter 6 14
Chapter 7 17
Chapter 8 19
Chapter 9 22
Chapter 10 30
Chapter 11 33
Chapter 12 35
Chapter 14 49
Chapter 15 53
Chapter 16 56
Chapter 17 58
Chapter 18 62
Chapter 19 64
Chapter 20 65
Chapter 21 66
Chapter 22 67
Chapter 23 69
Chapter 24 70
Chapter 25 76
Chapter 26 82
Chapter 27 86

Chapter 26	88
Chapter 27	95
Chapter 28	99
Chapter 29	104
Chapter 30	110
Chapter 31	112
Chapter 32	119
Chapter 33	126
Chapter 34	130
Chapter 35	136
Chapter 36	151
Chapter 37	154
Chapter 38	162
Chapter 39	176
Epilogue	177

Chapter 1

Charlie wasn't having a good time. *Fucking Catholics have the market cornered on wallowing in depression.* But it was a funeral after all. The ceremony was for Jennifer, his wife's long-time best friend. Margo was inconsolable, her massive boobs heaving in heartfelt grief. Of course, thinking of breasts reminded Charlie to casually glance over his shoulder at the statuesque, voluptuous unknown redhead in the pew behind them. *Wow,* he thought while somehow maintaining the appropriate facial expression of a mourner, *those things are as big as my head!*

But the oppressive stuffiness of the church, all the sobbing and the wailing kept him from really enjoying the chest heaving of all sizes and shapes around him. He cast his eyes down at the redhead's cleavage, pretending to wipe away tears, while he got a good, long look. At 60, his eyesight wasn't sharp enough to admire the whole presentation with just a quick glance; it took a couple minutes to drink it all in. He was starting to perk up enough to pat his wife's shoulder and rub her back. Of course, she thought he was getting frisky from sneaking peeks at the Amazon woman behind them and flashed him a disapproving frown.

Margo shouldn't have worried. The meds the doctor had put him on for his diabetes were making his (and her) sex life a fond and faint reminiscence like tight butt cheeks and his 28-inch waist he now hid behind a roll of fat. He loved sex and in honor of its on-again, off-again nature offered to "take care of her" on numerous occasions, but she gently rebuffed him, "I'm not getting off without you." He called it her act of righteous denial dying on the cross for his sins and he was infuriated for her unwanted sacrifice, a gesture that made him feel guilty and frustrated for no longer making her toes curl and giggle like a schoolgirl one more time.

In the beginning he thought a big, meaty girl like her would be needy and cloying, but she spouted wonderful, cool strong statements like, "Don't forget your condoms," when he was leaving town, almost daring him to fuck around. Of course, that was before any real understanding or commitment between them made itself known. It was before he moved in and got to know the cat.

Years later he resented her for not turning her back on him. *My God, woman. Have some pride!* He had cheated on her not once, not twice, but many times, wagging his member around town while it still worked on a consistent basis. When Margo had discovered the emails and cross-checked his cell calls, he was relieved to be found out. And just disgusted when she didn't kick him to the curb but instead took him back, first tentatively like he was on probation, then with a fierce need that translated into hot, nasty lust that threatened to consume them both.

She would come home in the middle of the day, and like in the movies, they'd rip off each other's clothes off and devolve into mindless, fucking animals. For about a week.

Sitting here in church lost in his daydreams, he noticed he was sporting a half-eager woody.

"Hello, old friend."

"Interesting title," the agent muttered. "Confessions of a Ladies Man." He gave Charlie the once-over.

"Fuck anybody famous?"

"No."

"Are you now or have you ever been famous?"

"No."

"Then who's going to buy your book?"

He felt Harvey's attention wavering.

"I've known famous people. We snorted coke together and bought each other Christmas presents."

"But you didn't fuck 'em?"

"No."

"Are they in the book?"

"No. That's another book."

Harvey tossed *Ladies Man* across the desk. "Then write *that* book, but shock me, make me feel every blowjob, every orgasm. Give me *50 Shades*. Women love that stuff."

Of course, Margo didn't know about his dalliance with her best friend. Jennifer was a nervous type; she almost took all the joy out of the affair.

She would run to her blinds every ten minutes.

"Are you *sure* Margo doesn't know?"

"Relax, baby cat," he'd say, borrowing a cute phrase he stole from a Hungarian friend.

She was petite, all sinew and bone, tiny breasts on a chest that flushed scarlet and gave away her passion when he nuzzled her neck. She had a runner's body that threatened to bolt every time her phone rang.

Jennifer's husband wasn't a consideration. She and Jim had run marathons together until three years before when he dropped dead just a block from the house.

"I found a full pack of Marlboros in his sock drawer," she whispered into Charlie's crotch not long after the funeral.

"The nerve of him," he consoled her. "Leaving such a hot little slut to fend for herself."

But a girl like Jennifer was high maintenance, especially when the three of them went out to dinner or played cards at his house. He carefully monitored her alcohol intake, always afraid she'd fall apart and confess everything in a sloppy, drunken funk.

He and Margo had fixed her up with Margo's tennis coach, Tony, a half-wit that played a mean game of tennis and cursed like a truck driver.

"I wonder how she can stand the words that come out of his mouth," Margo mused.

Don't worry, he thought, *she likes it just fine.*

They didn't stay long at the get-together after; Charlie lost interest when the Amazon redhead failed to show. Tony, he noticed, had put on some weight. He sat on the sofa, gazing off into the distance, barely acknowledging the platitudes and words of sympathy.

As they were leaving, Charlie went to say his goodbyes. Tony looked up and recognition came to his eyes.

"Jennifer told me about you. Fuck."

"Fuck, indeed," Charlie answered, not knowing if he was confessing or sharing Tony's pain. Maybe both.

Chapter 2

Charlie frowned down at his twitching thumb. The digit seemed to have a mind of its own, dancing back and forth as though shaking off a taxing game of *World of Warcraft*. He googled "twitching thumb" and agreed with the internet that the term "resting tremor" was an adequate description of his thumb's independent actions.

"…a possible symptom of early onset Parkinson's," the site explained. "Parkinson's," another site diagnosed. The Folk Doctor weighed in, "Could be Parkinson's."

Shit. That couldn't be good. He didn't know much about the disease. He remembered it was incurable. But he hadn't heard that PD had killed anybody. He googled it.

Neurological…gradual loss of nerve cells in the brain…

He saw Hilda, his masseuse, on Fridays and told her about his growing suspicions.

"Go check it out," she advised him. She gave him his Happy Ending like he liked it, no theatrics, matter-of-fact, business as usual. "Go to the doctor," she said as he stretched his arms over his head to work out the kinks.

He was going to, but he put it off for dinner with Kimberly, his new personal trainer. She didn't know a filet mignon from a Happy Meal so he didn't splurge. Margo called while they were eating. He excused himself. He needn't have bothered; Kim was busy checking her Instagram.

"When are you coming home? Should I hold up dinner?" He heard that clingy tone in Margo's voice.

"I'm at dinner right now with an old client," he explained.

Cold steel. "Right." The phone went silent.

"Hello?"

He wasn't sure she had hung up on him. Damn cell phones. In the old days you got dial tone in your ear when somebody hung up on you. Fuck her. Pretense was dead.

At the table, Kimberly had finished her salad and eyed his filet disapprovingly.

"Are you really going to eat that disgusting slab of red meat?"

"I'm going Vegan tonight, baby."

Sometimes corny and bold won the day and her smile was an invitation.

"My place or yours?" she asked already knowing the answer.

"Yours? Mine is getting uh, fumigated."

Her place was decorated in powder blue and pink pastels, just waiting for a baby shower. Kimberly caught his rueful assessment and dialed the lights down.

He sat on the living room sofa watching her undress for him while she watched him watching her. He turned around and saw a floor to ceiling mirror. Apparently, she was watching herself.

Her slinky black cocktail dress sparkled with sequins and slipped over her little b cups and down her thighs, pooling in a dark ring around her ankles. Off came her bra. And revealed a pair of perfect pert surgically enhanced breasts. A pair of black stockings drew a line between her garter belt, through the Promised Land, to her pink manicured toes. The black lace matched, accenting her alabaster skin. Her magnificent, muscular thighs flexed as she lifted each stilettoed foot out of her panties.

She planted one stilettoed foot in his lap, threatening to impale his impending erection. Her toenails seemed to glimmer in the pool of light cast by a lamp next to the sofa. He could feel the stirrings that announced the little blue pill was working.

"Any special requests, Charlie?"

"Your bed. Now."

Her clothes defined the path to her bedroom. He sat on the side of the bed as she unzipped his fly and pleasured him. He awkwardly shrugged out of his shirt and tie and focused on what she was doing to him, how good it felt, and tried like hell to avoid debilitating distraction.

Twenty years ago, I was reciting baseball stats in my head to keep from coming too soon. Now, I chase away any thoughts that make me lose focus – and my erection.

They fell back on her bed, his slacks still lashed to his ankles, held in place by his shoes. He reciprocated orally and breathed in her musky odor commingled with the last vestiges of a flowery scent.

Steady there, partner, he prayed to his semi-committed member, *we're on the ten-yard line and headed for the end zone.*

Charlie lunged, his head abruptly nestled between her pert young breasts and an even stronger scent of flowers. Kimberly was warm and moist, like a damp towel enveloping him. Her womb emanated heat like a furnace.

"Ooh, daddy! Ride me!"

"Oh yeah. Oh yeah!" he responded.

He hated dirty sex talk, this fornicating play-by-play. He was a grunt-and-groan guy. With Charlie it wasn't the journey, it was all about the destination.

She was getting close. She had switched to an undulating animal sound, and he predicted her orgasm and a crescendo were reaching the grand finale.

"Ah!" she gasped/shouted, like she had just discovered the cure for cancer. He continued to slam into her for wave upon wave until with a final shudder from her, he was sure she was satisfied. Then, gentleman that he was, he galloped into the home stretch for his own release.

But rather than the relief that came from an intense orgasm, a flash of heat roared up from the back of his head and seemed to explode from the top of his skull.

"Aaagh!" he screamed in pain.

She rolled out from under him and snapped on a bedside lamp.

"Oh my God! Your face is beet red! Should I call 9-1-1?"

"No! Just give me," he panted, "a minute. I'll be all right in a minute."

Already the pain was beginning to subside. Now it was a dull throb in his neck muscles.

He slowly rose and got dressed. Kimberly brought him some aspirin and a glass of water.

"Thanks." He headed toward the door and stopped. "I'm probably not going to be at the gym tomorrow."

She nodded. "Go see a doctor."

Chapter 3

Charlie had always wanted a woman doctor, but there were things he couldn't see confessing to a female: any venereal disease that threatened to make his dick fall off or an issue that kept him from rising to the occasion.

Old Doc James was a man's doctor, stinking of cigarettes and constantly bitching about his golf game. He had to be 70 at least and would probably die somewhere on the back nine.

"I'm going to run a bunch of tests to rule out just about everything," he told Charlie. He poked him in the stomach, "Chances are, though, with a gut like that, I'd say your diabetes is flaring up."

"What about the head explosion?"

"High blood pressure and I'd bet high cholesterol, too."

"You're a fucking barrel of laughs, doc."

"Treat your body like a toilet, Charlie, and it's going to back up on you."

"Maybe I should call a plumber."

"He'd probably charge you double."

"What about Parkinson's? The Internet doesn't lie."

"Nah. Don't even worry about it. I'll call you when I get the results."

"So, how's the Great American Novel coming?"

"How's this for a title: *Love in the Time of Viagra?*"

"What's it about?"

"Just kidding. Here's one: Pierre LaCrosse works in a 19th century perfumery. Most sensitive nose in Paris. But one particular scent sets him off and he kills the unfortunate woman wearing that brand."

"It could work. Give me a couple chapters."

For hours the blank screen stared back, mocking him.

That's me. Lots of ideas. No follow-through.

Chapter 4

His jokes today didn't cheer up Doc James like they usually did.

"Jesus, James. Smile and give it to me straight."

"I'm sending you to a neurologist. Everything on the internet points to Parkinson's."

"You just confirmed what I always knew about you quacks. You don't know any more than we do! I thought you said the problem was in my fuel ignition?"

"I'm not joking, Charlie." He handed him a card. "Go see Dr. Brain."

"Dr. Brain? Really?"

"It's just a name. Go see her, you idiot."

He received a call that afternoon.

"This is Doctor Brain's office. You have been scheduled with her next Tuesday."

"I don't remember calling the doctor or is that part of the disease?"

She ignored his joke. "Your attending physician made the appointment. We will see you next Tuesday."

Chapter 5

Dr. Brain spoke with a clipped British accent and had a mole on her forehead he tried to ignore.

"What makes you think you have Parkinson's?"

"I checked out a few websites and…"

"You do know you can't always rely on the internet for accurate information, right? Your friend Dr. James doesn't agree with your diagnosis."

He nodded.

She held up both of her hands and had him do the same.

"Now tap your index finger and your thumb together."

She watched as he tapped finger to thumb rapidly.

"Okay. Now turn around and walk down the hallway and back."

He casually strolled down the hall and back. He was beginning to think old Doc James and Dr. Brain were putting him on.

"You have Parkinson's."

"What?"

"Your gait and your right hand are stiffer, slower on the right than the left."

"How long before I need a wheelchair? How long before I die?"

"Good. You know it's an incurable disease and that you gradually get worse. And that more than likely, you will die with the disease but not from your disease."

"Again, how long…"

"Parkinson's symptoms are very individual. You could go years without the disease getting worse. Some live an otherwise normal life and a regular span of years."

"C'mon doc. I'm a big boy. Give me a worst-case scenario."

"Medical science is making all kinds of advances, Charlie... You can lose your memory, your body strength. It's a neurological disease. Basically, anything can happen. It's progressive, so in most cases it continues to get worse."

"Am I going to die?"

"Charlie, we're all going to die."

"Yeah, but sooner than later, right? I could walk out of here and get hit by a truck, but more than likely this fucking disease is going to kill me."

"The disease could advance enough to slow down and stiffen your stride and *then* you could get hit by that truck. Would friends say, 'The illness finally got him,' or 'Charlie got hit by a truck?'"

He was getting depressed with all this frankness.

"So, Dr. *Brain*, what are my options?"

She described several medicines as the first course of treatment.

"You also might consider Deep Brain Stimulation at some time, but that's way off."

She ran him through some cognitive tests.

"Remember these five words in no particular order: sunflower, church, red, cake, apple. I'll ask you to repeat them back to me later."

He drew the features of a clock on a circle and added the hands indicating it was 3:40. He identified a rhino. He counted backwards from 100 by seven.

"Can you tell me those five words?"

"What five words?" he grinned. "Rose, apple... Sunflower, rose, red... Sunflower, red, cake, apple, church."

"Good. We'll see you in three months."

Chapter 6

They had another one of their senseless, never-ending battles that same night. He was holding back the news of his diagnosis like an ace up his sleeve. *Man, will the guilt roll in!*

She had said no so many times, he was grateful that she was willing to make an attempt at sex. Then nothing happened. He was pissed that she was okay with his failure. He hated that veiled look of pity so much, he wanted to wipe it off her face *now*.

He was in full self-loathing mode. "I hate myself almost as much as you hate me! You treat me like shit and I keep coming back. No wonder you don't respect me!"

"I have never needed anybody and I'm not going to start now! You knew it when you got involved with me that I'm a very independent person."

She was right. No cuddling, no spooning. Foreplay was a couple of glasses of wine followed by frenzied unbuttoning, rough, sloppy French kisses and nipple pinches that felt more like an assault than a tender embrace. She shuddered and moaned as she came. The truth was he needed her.

Five times that first encounter, tying his record with any previous girlfriend. But then four years ago he was diagnosed with diabetes. The medicine robbed him of a decent erection and his manhood no longer spontaneously rose to the occasion when called upon to perform.

They were lying there next to each other, not touching, frustrated.

"Why don't you let me play with your boobs anymore? You used to love that."

"It's hot. I'm sweaty."

Silence.

"And I didn't like it all that much. I never have. They're not as sensitive as the little ones are."

"But I played with them for hours. You 'oohed' and 'aahed.'"

"You were enjoying yourself."

So, it was not a surprise when she announced she was seeking a breast reduction.

"Why?" he asked, his voice caught between grief and a petulant whine.

"Since we've been together, they've grown from double Ds to a saggy F."

He knew; he figured they had flourished in appreciation of his nurturing worship.

"I love your tits."

"The sheer weight of them is killing my back."

He would have been happy carrying them around for her and told her so.

"Is that why you love me? Don't you care about my health?"

He said, "No and yes" when the answer was really closer to "Yes, that's why he loved her and yes, he cared about her health" if it meant she was keeping them intact.

He went with her for her pre-op with the plastic surgeon. The surgeon was in his thirties, maybe 6'5", 230 pounds, probably a solid defensive back in college.

The doctor asked her to open her gown to assess the job ahead. Charlie studied the surgeon's face for any unprofessional reaction. He was quiet on the way home.

"Well?" she asked.

"You know how I feel," he said. "Did you see the way he openly drooled?"

She rolled her eyes. "He must see 30 pairs a day. I'm sure it's just a job for him."

"How do you know he didn't go into that profession just to stare and touch 30 pairs of boobs a day? Hell, they wouldn't even have to pay me. And I can't imagine growing bored with fondling them all day."

He paused to reload his critical onslaught. "How old is he anyway? What kind of grades did he get before he graduated, what, two years ago?"

"Stop it! I'm doing this. You can be supportive or not."

"Just let him know if he fucks this up, I'll kill him."

The surgery lasted three hours. He had waited it out in the waiting room, looking at porn sites on his phone like hugetits.com and www.massivebreasts. He was officially in mourning.

He tried his best not to look mortified when she showed him what the surgeon had done. Angry stitches ran across her mounds both vertically and horizontally. He had used her beautiful caramel colored, dollar-sized areolas as miniature roundabouts, and had cut them down to the size of quarters or maybe even nickels. *Welcome to the R rated version of Bride of Frankenstein.*

"How long before she can, you know?" he asked the doctor.

"Six to eight weeks."

"I don't want you hanging around, moping. Why don't you get out of town for a while?" she suggested. "You suck as a caretaker so I have already asked for my sister to come out."

"In that case I think I'll book something now."

But first, he was going to try mending a few fences.

Chapter 7

Randy had an uncanny ability to reach out at the right moments: leaving the party just before the cops showed, suggesting Charlie drop his stock in Braniff Airlines just before they declared bankruptcy, and hiding their 20 kilos with another friend hours before the DEA raided their house and found nothing. He was the only link back to the days after graduation from Boys and Girls High School in Brooklyn.

"Thanks for calling, Randy. Actually, I was about to call you."

"So, what's up?" Randy asked.

"I'm going to Thailand next week. Want to make it a buddy trip?"

"Man! I wished I had called you earlier. I would love to go!"

"A week's notice, two months. It doesn't matter with you. You're always working."

"Yeah, but I'm in court for at least three weeks. The prosecutor is gorgeous and we have to go to lunch a lot."

"Carpe diem, my friend. Although I admit you have found a way to balance this work/play time, if it's about the sex, you could do that in Bangkok. Without the court time. I swear, Randy, you're going to approach the bench one of these days for the last time."

"I do like the lady boys. Give me a few hours to see if I can rearrange my workload."

"Great! I hate to get into trouble alone."

Three hours later, Randy called back and face-timed him.

Charlie was looking at a lot of skin. "Wait a minute. Are you naked?"

"Yeah, just got out of the shower. You like?"

"Not my cup of tea."

"I'm just calling to say sorry, dude. Can't do it. But kiss a lady boy for me, okay?"

"You know I'm straight, right?" Charlie was clearly flustered.

"Leave yourself open to all the possibilities. You're on a quest, a hedonistic quest, granted, but feel free to explore."

"How do you figure I'm on a quest?"

"You've got those sad puppy dog eyes, so I'd say it's a health issue, right?"

For some reason, he didn't want to divulge his condition to this particular old friend.

"Stop the analysis. You nailed it. I've got a headache listening to you trying to analyze me. Or seduce me. Or whatever that was." Here was his opportunity to share what was really going on. "I'm dy…"

Randy sighed. "I guess you'll always be, deep down, a homophobe. And a jerk. I'm hanging up now."

"Wait!" he groaned. Would this be their last conversation ever?

He tried to call him back. Tried ten times, but Randy wouldn't pick up. He always retreated to recover from perceived slights. He would be unapproachable for 48-72 hours. And, if he was working, it could be longer because now it became an inconvenience.

Chapter 8

He called his old best friend Arthur. He was a tall, skinny African-American from way, way back. If he and Randy went back to the Vietnam War, he and Arthur knew each other during the Jurassic era or at least elementary school. His Texas years.

Arthur Briggs could pick up any musical instrument and, within 15 minutes of fooling around with it, play a recognizable tune. Back in the day they were neighbors, both from the wrong side of the tracks in a time and place Charlie thought he'd left behind.

"I don't know how you tracked me down, but I'm glad you did."

"We have a lot of catching up to do. About 40 years' worth."

"Let me just get one thing off my chest. What's left of it."

"What?"

"Desert Storm. We just missed Vietnam and I was ready to go. Locked and loaded. Psyched myself into it and Nixon shut the thing down. Then, I thought after 9-11 I owed the country something. Turns out it was an arm and a leg. And COPD."

"Shit, Arthur, I'm sorry."

"Can't put a trumpet to my lips and the sax sets me to wheezing."

"So why are you glad I called?"

"You were a mean little cracker. We were friends until the rich white boys came around. At the first sign they were going to let you into their little circle, you couldn't hang with me."

"I'm so sorry, Arthur. I never realized. I searched my memory and thought we just drifted apart. It's a shitty thing to do. How can I make it up to you?"

"You just did. That little 'sorry' took a load off my mind. Praise Jesus."

"I could take you to Thailand."

"You should have figured out by now that my international days of travel are over. Besides, ain't you got any other friends?"

"I don't have many guy friends anymore."

"So, being an asshole is now a full-time thing?"

"Pretty much." Charlie took a deep breath.

"Arthur, I'm dying."

"I'm still not going with you to Thailand."

"No. Really. I've got Parkinson's."

"How long you got?"

"There's no way to know. Each case is different."

"Is there a chance this is the worst it gets?"

'Yeah, it's a possibility."

"Bad times ahead?"

"Memory loss, painful body cramps, hallucinations, dementia. There's more."

A long moment of silence followed.

"Want to pray about it?"

"What have I got to lose?"

Arthur resumed in hushed tones.

"Please bow your head. Heavenly father, we call on you to help my friend, Charlie. He's making his way back to you now, lord. Give him peace. Amen."

"Not very upbeat, was it?"

"He already forgave you. If you accept him as your savior, you get a ticket to heaven. What more do you want?"

"A miracle."

"Sometimes we fail to see that we are victims of our own making."

"Yeah, all that 'reap what you sow' bullshit. I'm not feeling comforted, not feeling saved. Just not feeling it. Nice talking to you, Arthur. Sorry about your fucked-up life. Good luck. I mean it."

Charlie hung up and for a minute he just stared at his phone like he was expecting a call from Jesus.

Maybe he was on the right path, wrong religion.

He was halfway to Bangkok when he realized he hadn't told Margo he was dying.

Chapter 9

His buddy Boon met him at the airport in Bangkok at 4:30 AM. Boon spoke very little English and Charlie spoke even less Thai, so they drove in relative silence the three hours to Pattaya to a modest motel near the beach. Some Buddhists have a term, *esho funi,* you and your environment are one. Charlie looked at the concrete walls that had gone from white to gray with tiny cracks like varicose veins. It was seedy, aged by the decadent things that had occurred under its roof. Yep, they belonged together.

"Tomorrow night I bring you friend," Boon said.

He slept off his jet lag and woke at early twilight. Alone in the city, Charlie ventured tentatively from the hotel and found a two-story neighborhood of homes above shops. Alleys were almost as busy as the streets with loud traffic. Smoky tuk tuks mingled with dirt bikes threatening to mow him down, advancing on him like angry insects. Taxis flew by with urgent business, and the diesel smell of buses carried local Thais home from work, windows open, riders breathing in their own exhaust.

There were stalls all along the main street. He dodged across four lanes of traffic to a stand with indescribable pieces of meat and noodles displayed in a cabinet next to a huge wok. The smells made him realize how hungry he was. He pointed to some items.

"One hundred baht," the seller asked, an old man with a face etched with wrinkles. He wore a faded New York Yankees t-shirt.

That was about three bucks. "Mai paan!" (Not expensive.)

Charlie had forgotten how sultry the nights were here. Actually, the days were too. He found a 7-11 and bought two big bottles of

Chang beer. He flagged down a tuk tuk.

"Here's one hundred baht. Just drive me around till the cash runs out." He handed the appreciative driver one of the beers and opened the other for himself. He was afraid to think about what he was breathing in. Tuk tuks were basically a cart attached to a motorcycle, one wheel in front, two in the back. Built low to the ground, they could weave in and out of traffic and turn sharp corners to avoid pedestrians and other vehicles. They also caught most of the exhaust from everyone on the road.

He finished his beer and asked the driver to drop him off for a cheap massage. It was a Buddhist temple that ran a massage school. A deluxe two-hour massage would run him about $20 US. She didn't speak a lick of English, but she was good, kneading his limbs with strong hands. Not much to look at, but he was there to get the kinks out.

"Do you, you know?" He made the universal gesture for a hand job.

She turned red, rose and left the room. She came back with an older woman. "Sir, you are in a holy place. There are plenty of places in Bangkok to receive the services you're looking for. Please leave."

"Look, I'm sorry if I offended the little lady. Can we just finish the job?"

"Sir, please leave."

They tried to return his money. "Keep it."

He found the kind of place he was looking for just around the corner. Even at three times the amount, the price was reasonable.

Back at the hotel, there was a Thai woman waiting for him at the front desk. She turned to the desk clerk to translate.

"Are you Mr. Charlie?"

"Chai. Yes," he replied.

Saowopa was her name, a pretty common Thai name, for an uncommon woman. She was Thai with some Chinese ancestry that made her look exotic in a land of exotic-looking women and men. Her nose wasn't a distinctive Thai nose; it was narrower. She dressed in western wear, distressed jeans and a silky top, but with practical shoes for running after tuk tuks and taxis.

Charlie, captivated, suddenly realized Boon stood behind her. They climbed into his car and drove just a few blocks. "Good place," Boon offered. The three of them sat sipping beers at a restaurant on the beach and watched the tide turning inward under a full moon.

She was about 5'6", a confident Thai woman with mischief dancing in her eyes. She joked with the waiter in Thai.

"You seem like a woman of the world," Charlie ventured.

"Why?"

"Because you're so…"

"Why?"

"That's all the English you know, isn't it?"

"Hello."

After dinner, Boon dropped them off at his hotel. The lively little hotel bar overflowed in the early evening with Thai and Japanese businessmen and the occasional American expat. Men gravitated to Saowopa's orbit, more than willing to do her bidding, attentive to her every whim, but she made Charlie feel like he was in on the joke. When she accepted their offer of a drink, she insisted they buy him one, too.

He tried typing a sentence into his phone's translator app, having her type one in return, a conversation conducted in slow motion. She could be brainless or a genius, but the barrier of language and the excruciatingly slow back and forth conducted through his phone made her a mystery. She wasn't hot or ravishingly beautiful, but she had an engaging laugh and a smile that sucked him right in. He was smitten.

She was haughty with her countrymen, able to swap stories and throw back drink for drink till the wee hours of the morning, but he would turn and find her taking another countless selfie with him in the background.

"Want to come up and spend the night?" he asked her at closing time.

"Why?"

"Because I want to have my way with you."

"Why?"

She spent the night but refused to share his bed. She curled up on the sofa fully dressed.

The next morning Boon met them out front for the three-hour drive to Bangkok. Pattaya had been a disappointment. The city was much more depressing than the last time he had visited. The streets were filled with old, fat white men with young or middle-aged Thai women. He asked Boon, "Doesn't it bother you that farang come and screw your women?"

He shrugged. "They both get something from it."

Saowopa was so sweet to him, giving him back rubs from the back seat of the car, anticipating his needs, flashing the kind of dazzling smile that fuels a schoolboy crush. *Does she like me? Is she interested? What if she is?* He thought about Margo and felt a pang of guilt. *You can't fix what's broken by breaking someone else. Peace comes from within.* Being around Buddhists all day was turning him into a fucking philosopher. But Thailand hadn't cured his Erectile Dysfunction; it mocked him several times a day with come-hither looks from dainty flowers lounging outside the massage parlors and the nasal taunts of bar girls ringing in his ears.

After a few drinks, she was a little more expressive, seemed to know a little more English.

"I'd love to make love to you," he growled.

"Why?"

He imagined how he'd write about her later.

Saowopa was a little feral (unpolished), her emotions raw and exposed (with no social graces). And bruised (blunt). And obviously wary of anything resembling a relationship with a here-today-gone-tomorrow non-Thai farang. That's the love story he spun for himself. This was stuff that was going in the book. Maybe.

They found a bar near the hotel the next night, a place with loud Thai rock n roll. Boon argued with a tuk tuk driver for a cheaper fare and ignored Saowopa and Charlie as they flirted back and forth in broken English. Loud music drowned out what each might have heard, but Boon picked up all the signals as they touched and smiled at each other. He had seen it every night for his entire 38 years. Americans, Europeans, the Japanese, they were all the same. His American friend seemed to be enjoying Saowopa's company. Charlie grinned and couldn't stop. She ordered round after round and teased him, pretending to brush up against him, letting him drape his arm around her like she was his.

Of course, back in his room nothing happened. He squeezed her breasts as she lay under him with no reaction from her. He loosened his belt and his pants fell. His penis seemed to be in a phallic form of a fetal position, curled into itself and so small and helpless and oh, so hopeless. But he was a gentleman. He would take care of her needs. He moved to do his part.

"Why?" she asked, not in a meaningful way. It was just one of the words she used with confidence and repeated like an inquisitive five-year-old.

"Best question I've heard all day."

She lay on her side. He spooned against her back, reached around and cupped a breast. He listened to her breathing slow and give in to slumber.

"I love you," he whispered, not really believing it, but trying to feel something.

All-in-all, over the following week there were six bars, six massages, six failures.

"I love you," he repeated often. She smiled and asked, "Why?"

It was a valid question.

Don't try to carry on a conversation with two Thais in the car when you're the only farang. Saowapa had stayed behind in Pattaya. Boon and Chakrii, a friend catching a ride back with them, prattled on for hours, ignoring him and only occasionally letting him on what they were talking about. The advantage? Lots of time in his head to mull things over: the real reason that a pretty girl is so attentive, do they only like music with Thai lyrics, how much does it cost to ship a body that's been cremated first?

First question: She calls you "daddy" because she doesn't know the more dismissive term "Pops."

Second: How many non-English songs do you hear on American radio? Thais are making their own music. We just didn't notice.

An urn is significantly cheaper than a casket due to the substantial weight difference.

They were careening toward Bangkok in traffic that was heavy but moving at about 60 miles per hour when he threw his car door open impulsively. Trying to pitch himself headlong into the path of afternoon delivery trucks and taxis he prayed they wouldn't be able to stop in time to avoid running over him. He forgot to unlatch his seatbelt; it hugged him tightly as the car door swung back and slammed into his fingers. Boon frowned, annoyed and temporarily distracted from a more interesting animated conversation on his cell phone. Charlie, fingers throbbing, felt like an asshole. An unsuccessful asshole.

"You like an uncle," she had said to him this morning over breakfast, "Not a sexy boyfriend."

He was a stud once, with bedroom eyes and a grin that melted hearts. He always got the girl. He could, and often would, have whoever he wanted. And so what. *Some third-world whore rebuffs me and I want to kill myself?* Even he recognized he was overreacting to her rejection. It was his vanity, his ego that wanted to blame her for not being interested. She wasn't a whore. *He was the one who had read into every touch, every smile.* If she were here now he would apologize, but Saowopa was in the rearview mirror and next week she would probably be cheering up some other loser.

To celebrate his return to Bangkok, Charlie took his friend for a two-hour massage. Charlie had developed a taste for Thai massage over the years. Before, his favorite had been Swedish. The masseuse kneads the muscles, working out the stored tension until you feel like a bowl of melted butter. A Thai masseuse will twist the customer into a pretzel, wringing out the tension like a washcloth, leaving you limp and spent. But in his experience, only Thai massage promised a "Happy Ending."

After their massage, Boon showed him a sushi bar where there was no comparison to quality or price between Bangkok and New York. They drank sake into the wee hours, leaving self-pity, also, in the rearview mirror.

"Boon, do you know a Buddhist priest who speaks English?"

The English school was located on temple grounds just above the parking lot. The heat of the day gave the new asphalt a spongy feel to their walk. He was paying 30 baht to meet with the monk and pick through his metaphysical knowledge to answer his questions.

The monk was western looking despite his saffron robe, his hair closely cropped appropriately.

"I'm Henry. Welcome to our temple."

He gave Charlie a tour, explaining the differences between the Buddhism practiced in Thailand with that of China, Japan, or the other countries that follow the teachings of Buddha.

"You know," he informed Charlie, "They say there are 30,000 sutras or teachings, 30,000 possible interpretations of those teachings, leading to 30,000 sects of Buddhism. I was a Nichiren Buddhist in my teens, a Zen Buddhist in my twenties, now here I am."

"So this is it?" asked Charlie. "This is the one?"

"I don't know. Sixty-four million Thais think so. I'm headed to Tibet next week."

"Do you guys, or rather, *those* guys, believe in a Heaven and a Hell?

"There are basically four worlds: hell, with eights levels, then there's our world, one level. Then there are six levels of heaven and 16 levels in the place that's greater than heaven."

"Greater than heaven? I want to go there!"

"*You* can't go there. Buddhism says there is no self, no soul."

"What? So there really isn't anything in it for me?"

"There's like a little flame of you inside that has collected your karma from this existence and past existences to this current form. Will it still be you when "you" are gone? Theories differ, but the Theravada school says no. But, on a good note, rebirth is immediate."

"So, we skip Heaven at that point and start over? As what?"

"We've got the six realms. You can return as a heavenly god, a demigod, a human, an animal, a ghost, or a creature of hell. Where you end up is all based on your karma. Eventually, it's hoped that each of us will reach nirvana. That's your ticket off the endless cycle of rebirth."

"How do I get there?"

"You have to stop your hunger and desire and follow the eight-fold path. You must learn to discipline your mind and body and practice mindfulness and meditation."

"How long does this take?"

"For most, many lifetimes."

"But it's not me, right? It's my little flame?"

"Very perceptive! You catch on quickly!"

"Please don't feed my ego!"

The priest applauded his insight.

"Are you ready to join us, brother?" the excited monk asked him.

"Thanks, but I've got a lot of desires to unload. After that, I have to achieve mindfulness and discipline. Then there's meditation, sitting for hours and looked inward. Isn't the urge to be a better human being just another way of clinging to desire?"

"I've never looked at it that way before," said Henry in awe.

"Thanks, Henry. I hate to sound shallow, but I'm looking for a quicker fix. I'll try it your way next time."

"Try the Catholics," the monk shouted after him.

Chapter 10

Charlie found a Catholic church in the middle of Bangkok, something of a historical artifact from western civilization, a stiff, austere building that stood out among the great white Buddhist temples, still busy and still listening to the congregation's confessions. Charlie stared up at the Asian-looking Jesus nailed to the cross as he approached a young-looking Thai priest. *"Funny, you don't look Jewish."*

"Excuse me, do you have anyone who speaks English?"

"I do."

"Can you take my confession?"

"Well, first of all, we don't take your confession. It's not dictation. We receive your confession on God's behalf." The young priest looked him over.

"You're not Catholic. Why are you here?"

"Like everyone else, father, I'm looking for answers."

"'Why am I here?' that sort of thing?"

"That and so much more."

"How much time do you have?"

"Ah! That's the question in the foremost of my mind!"

"You're not going to find answers on a two-week vacation. Or maybe you will. Who am I to say?"

"If you're going to be vague and cryptic, father, neither of us will get much out of this conversation."

The priest gesture to the confessional.

"Perhaps it's time to determine a course."

They stepped inside their respective compartments. The priest slid the window open.

"Bless me, father, for I have sinned."

"How so?"

"I have lied, cheated, fornicated out of wedlock, blas, uh blasphemed, goddamn it, cussed daily."

"Tell me, son. Do you understand the concept of penance?"

"I think so. I regret the bad shit I've done and will make it up somehow."

"Very good. Do you understand the concept of sinning, because it seems to me you're unclear on what it means to sin."

"Bad shit, excuse me, bad things that violate the Ten Commandments."

"Son, what faith were you born into?"

"Jewish. Not really a practicing Jew. Just sort of Jew-ish."

"Are you attached to a synagogue, a rabbi, somebody who can explain things in a way that speaks to you?"

"They're not there for *me*, father, I'm the bad guy."

"Nonsense. Satan is the bad guy. You're just somebody who is searching for the Truth."

"Does the Truth exist, father?"

"Just between you and me, hell if I know. I'm just a Jesuit trying to get to Heaven. Thoreau said one world at a time. You may not find The Answer, but you may find something that resonates with you, that provides you solace in the middle of the night or at death's door."

"But am I really Jewish? Just because I was born into the religion, surrounded by the culture? Will it save my rotten soul?"

"Are you a Yankee fan because you grew up in the Bronx? Are you a Republican because you were raised that way?"

The priest exited the vestibule and continued the conversation.

"Somewhere along the line we must define ourselves, figure out our moral code. Some of us carry on in the family tradition, content in our inherited convictions, never questioning our faith, never considering the possibility of a separate, equally true religion."

He clasped Charlie on the shoulder, trying to convey compassion.

"Peace be with you, brother. May your quest for answers yield results that fill your soul and erase any doubt. May it bring you solace."

"Thanks, father. Not The Answer, but an answer, nonetheless."

"See you in the next life," the priest said with a wink.

Chapter 11

He called Margo. Her shit sister, Peggy, answered.

"What do you want?"

"I wanted to find out if it's okay to come home yet. Obviously, it's not."

"What, so you can come on to me again?"

"Peggy, that was a mistake. One I regret every day."

"What's that supposed to mean?"

"I'm a changed man. I'm trying to turn over a new leaf."

"In your case, you would have to turn over a whole new tree."

Thank God that wasn't funny. It would hurt him to hate her while appreciating her comedic prowess.

"Can I talk to Margo? Please?"

"She's not here."

"Please let her know I called. By the way, how long are you staying?"

"Can't really say. My sister really needs me."

"Thanks for being there for her. I really mean it. Shame about the tits, though."

"Asshole." She disconnected.

"Hello?" he asked into the phone. No response. *Just want to make sure she actually hung up.*

All right, then. He wasn't headed home. He checked his frequent flyer miles then scrolled through his contacts. Brahim would have a shit ton of hashish waiting for him and could be persuaded to take Charlie to the liquor store.

Brahim was happy to hear from him. "You are coming to Morocco, yes?"

"Yes."
"No hotel; you are staying with me."
"Okay."
"Okay. See you soon."

Chapter 12

Brahim picked him up from Casablanca airport. Charlie gritted his teeth when they came to the roundabout at the city's edge. It was Friday and cars bumped and scratched each other coming into Casablanca. A lot of yelling and gesticulating was involved. Two drivers seemed very heated.

"What are they saying?" he asked his friend.

"Very politely one says, 'Excuse me, I do believe I had the right-of-way, but I could be mistaken.' The other says, "You may be right. Let us confer with a police officer."

"Yeah, right," Charlie scoffed. They both burst out laughing.

"Where is Margo?" asked Brahim.

"Who's Margo?"

The rest of the trip to Rabat should have been spent in silence, but Brahim's phone buzzed constantly and when he answered the conversation was conducted loudly in hostile tones.

After one such exchange, Charlie asked, "What was that all about?"

"What was what all about?"

"Point taken."

"Charlie, are you hungry?"

"I could eat a horse."

"Will camel meat be all right?"

"I was joking."

"So was I. Though you shouldn't knock it till you try it."

"Noura has prepared dinner for us."

Oh good, Noura was a great cook.

They arrived and Brahim dropped Charlie and his luggage in front of his building. It could take him five minutes or a half hour to find street parking in this area. Noura buzzed him up and he climbed the three flights to be greeted by Brahim's girlfriend and the smells of freshly-prepared tagine.

In a lot of ways, Noura was old-fashioned. No big hugs, but kisses delivered on both cheeks and a warm, welcoming smile. She wore western jeans and a colorful blouse.

Brahim came in panting.

"How far away did you have to park?" Charlie asked.

"Not too far. Four blocks."

"My god! You're practically at the beach."

"My car has a very pleasant view. Perhaps tomorrow morning we can take our coffee to my parking place and watch the sun rise together."

Brahim showed him where he would sleep. His room was long and narrow with sofas lining both sides and large, intricate artwork incorporating words from the Quran and a window that opened up to shout at street vendors as they passed below.

Charlie wanted to call his wife, but it was 4:00 am in New York and he wasn't sure he was ready.

They ate the tagine in traditional style; Charlie sat on his left hand to force himself to eat only with his right. They gave you a pass when you weren't from there, but he always went total Moroccan. The left hand was for wiping your ass, the right for shaking hands and eating dinner. He already looked at his left hand with disdain, but it was the right one that really betrayed him, shaking when he wasn't looking.

He breathed in the ingredients of the tagine: chicken surrounded by slices of potato, onion, carrots, tomatoes, herbs, bay leaf, ginger, garlic, drops of lemon and olive oil and saffron. This smell, to him, was the essence of Morocco. They finished the meal with pieces of fruit and Moroccan "whiskey," a mint tea that was usually much too sweet.

It wasn't until then that Brahim brought out the hash and the hookah. The hookah looked like a child's toy. *Is it a child's toy?* "*Happy birthday, son. Here's your starter hookah!*"

"No, my friend. This water pipe is for serious business. Adults only."

Brahim turned to Noura and said something in Arabic. She left the room.

"She doesn't partake. I told her I would see her tomorrow."

Ten minutes later he was really stoned, eyes red and at half-mast.

"What time is it?"

"10:56 PM."

"What time would that be in New York?"

He really wanted to know, but he didn't want to turn on his long-distance plan to find out from Siri what time it was in New York. Besides, he had to save his minutes for actual conversations when he did reach her.

He already knew he was too stoned to talk to her at the moment. Or the next couple of hours. He and Brahim mumbled at each other, their limbs heavy. He would deal with that shit in the brilliance and promise of a new day. Yeah, right.

He woke at 10 am ready to call. He really wanted to make some peace with her. When he walked out on his advertising job to write the next great novel, she supported them both, never complaining about how he locked himself away to chase his muse. Or that it took him two years and he was still at it. In his travels he had neglected to put anything to paper.

"Hi, Peggy. It's me again."

"She's not here, Charlie."

"I'll keep trying."

"It has only been three weeks. The doctor said six to eight to heal. That means I'm going to be here a while."

"Okay. Thanks, Peggy."

"What, no smartass comeback?"

"Not today. See ya."

He hadn't realized he had dropped off again till Brahmin woke him an hour later.

"Come on, my friend. You need a cleanse."

The neighborhood hammam was just two blocks away. As usual, there were two entrances, one per gender. Cold water, lots of it, was thrown against the yellow tiles that covered every surface of the hammam. The cold water made the heat of the hammam tolerable, but it still threatened to suffocate him if he stayed in one room took long. He lay his face, left cheek pressed to the floor, to feel the tiny breeze as the caretaker scrubbed every inch of his exposed skin with black soap till it was raw.

This was a local hammam rarely frequented by strangers, especially by a chunky 60-year-old Jewish guy in his bathing suit.

A year before on his first trip to the hammam, he had stripped off all his clothes and wrapped his towel around his waist. The older guys threw stern frowns his way. Others avoided looking in his general direction.

"Don't leave that thing wagging about," Brahim hissed at him. "You're embarrassing me."

Funny people. Guys will hold hands, kiss each other, but don't you dare show your putz!

Charlie left the hammam, as always, feeling as though his pores were wide open. He felt every whisper of air pass over his body.

"Let's get breakfast," suggested Brahim. "You're buying."

They sat eating khlea, the closest thing to bacon in this Muslim country, and fried eggs, over easy. *Their friggin' eggs were always over easy.* The restaurant was small and loud passionate conversations flooded the place with noise.

"What brings you to Morocco this time, my friend?"

"I wasn't welcome at home."

"You know you are always welcome here."

Charlie nodded.

"But you should go home at your earliest convenience."

"My wife got her tits chopped off!"

"What!"

"Okay. Maybe I'm exaggerating a little."

"Oh my. Please explain." Brahim looked seriously earnest.

Brahim ordered more tea. "Strong."

His emotional reaction made Charlie see Margo's surgery in a new light.

"Margo's back was always hurting so she lightened the load, so to speak."

"Allah put those there, my friend, for you to enjoy. Of course, she asked your permission?"

"Yes, but she didn't really need it. She wanted my support."

"Did she have it?"

"Reluctantly."

"My friend, your problems are minor."

"Did I mention I'm dying?"

Concern etched Brahim's face. "What? Now? Are you in pain?"

"No. It's nothing right now. A little stiffness, muscle aches. Later. It's incurable."

"So we have some time, yes? What would you like to do today? Where would you like to go?"

"I would like to understand what your religion says of dying. Do you think there's something in that book of yours? Or should I go find a religious leader? Can you refer me to somebody?"

"If you would like to ask me the questions, you may. Or we could find somebody who knows a bit more. More tea?"

"But you're not actually a holy man, right?"

"No, but I have studied. You might consider me before pursuing the answers from strangers."

"Okay," Charlie decided. "You're obviously a devout Muslim. Let's give it a shot: What happens when I die?"

"Ah! Good one!" Brahim collected his thoughts. "Death isn't

'The End.' Life continues in another form."

"Like Buddhism?"

"No. This life is a test."

"Oh. Shit."

"This life is just a gateway to the afterlife when you will be judged."

"I'm screwed according to Islam."

"The good news is you're still alive. You can still do good deeds."

"Okay, I'm lying there on my deathbed, I've accomplished way more good deeds than bad. Then what?"

"Your last words in this world should be, 'I testify that there is no god but Allah, and Muhammad is the messenger of Allah.'"

"What if I'm zonked, out of it due to the painkillers?"

"If I am there I promise I will whisper those words in your ear."

Charlie looks at Brahim's sincere smile. "Thank you, my friend. But what about my seventeen virgins?"

"Seventy-two."

"What?"

"Plus all the women you ever married here on earth. All with appetizing vaginas. And you will have an eternal erection."

"Not if all my exes are around."

"Pray that the quantity of your good deeds is sufficient or your soul will be ripped from your body and cast into hell until Judgment Day. I'm afraid that will be your ultimate fate because you have not surrendered to Allah!"

Charlie's cell phone suddenly announced itself.

"Hello?"

"Charlie, it's Margo. Peggy said you were trying to reach me. Is this important?"

"Oh God, yes. We have to talk."

"Go ahead."

"Face to face. I'm in Morocco. I can be home in two days."

"Just a minute." She muffled the phone and had a brief conversation with her sister.

"Make it a week. Peggy's not leaving till next Saturday. And she would rather not see you."

The feeling's mutual.

"All right. I understand. I love you."

There was silence and a deep sigh from the other end then a longer silence that meant she had hung up without saying "I love you" back.

"Brahim, how far away is Tiznit? I'd like to buy some jewelry."

"Only six hours as the camel flies."

Charlie gave the obligatory chuckle. *Everybody's a comedian.*

Charlie watched as the scenery outside the car rolled by. The view changed from rolling, craggy hills and people everywhere to dusty roads and countryside which gave way to more gentle plains. Groves of argan trees dotted the landscape. Up ahead a solitary figure headed toward them. Brahim pulled over.

He wore a ragged djellaba that marked him as a farmer, but the smell of livestock identified him as a shepherd. He leaned in the car window to speak with Brahim in a slower, less heated exchange than the conversations Charlie heard in the cities. Charlie took in the shepherd's dirt-encrusted fingernails, his tobacco-stained teeth. He could have been 30 or 50.

"Salaam Aleichem!" Charlie's Moroccan vocabulary was limited, less then Thai, even.

"Aleikem salaam."

"He says he is going to Chefchouen, the Blue City. He humbly asks for a ride."

"Is he bringing his goats with him?"

"He is a sheep herder."

"Sorry. My mistake. Where is the Blue City from here?"

"About one hour that way." Brahim pointed back the way they had come. He saw Charlie's brow start to furrow.

"It would be a great kindness, a very good deed."

"Shit. Okay. Hop in!"

The shepherd smiled and patted his heart in thanks.

Brahim said something to him in Arabic.

The shepherd gave Charlie a sidelong glance and the two laughed, obviously sharing a joke.

"What was that about?" he asked Brahim.

"Uh, he was surprised you have never been to Chefchouen."

"Yeah, right."

The silence was dissipated by animated conversation. Charlie didn't pretend to follow the conversation. After Thailand, he didn't care.

"So why are you going to Chefchouen?" Charlie realized he was asking the wrong person. "Why is he going to Chefchouen?"

Brahim caught the eye of the shepherd in the rearview mirror and exchanged a couple sentences in another language. It wasn't Arabic or French.

"My Berber is a little rusty, but I think he said his name is Omar and he's going to get his wife."

Charlie couldn't tell if he was looking for a wife or had misplaced his. He didn't bother to ask further.

They were climbing the steep Rif Mountains now, almost there. The temperature outside had plummeted enough to chill him.

Omar directed them to a modern looking hospital.

Brahim said, "He says his wife is here."

Brahim and Charlie followed the shepherd as he frantically looked about for someone in charge. Family members, a middle-aged woman, another shepherd who was her apparent husband, and a man who appeared to be in his 20s, came running over to console him. The young man seemed interested in who they were. He and Brahim exchanged a few words before Brahim turned to Charlie with a shocked expression.

"His wife is dead! He's here to pick up her body."

"Oh my God! The family probably wants to be alone to grieve. Shouldn't we go?"

Another short intense conversation, this time with the sheepherder, Omar.

"The family would be honored if we stayed for the funeral. Omar is very grateful because we got him here so quickly."

"I guess it's okay," Charlie replied. "Is it okay? I mean, I'm not Muslim."

"In Morocco you are now family. We will follow them and the body to his wife's sister's home where they will prepare her for burial."

The family loaded Omar's wife's body, covered in a simple white sheet, gently into a cart pulled by a donkey. Omar, his brother-in-law and his nephew, followed by his quietly sobbing sister-in-law, kept pace with the cart.

An older woman and a younger one, the only person in the family he had seen in western garb, followed the men inside as they reverently carried the body into the house. Only Omar stayed inside with the women to prepare the body. The other men stayed outside, nervously smoking and murmuring to each other.

A few minutes later, the younger woman came out with a large carafe of hot mint tea, and a dozen small cups for the men.

"What is happening inside?" Charlie asked Brahim.

"They are washing the body, preparing her for burial."

Another half-hour passed before the men were called back in to pick up the shepherd's wife.

The women clustered at one side of the courtyard while the men gathered a few yards away. As they stood awaiting the imam, more men and women joined the gathering. Charlie was surprised to see a small handful of Orthodox Jews garbed in black. The original group of men carried the shepherd's wife out solemnly, silently, and deposited her body, shrouded in white, back onto the cart without the donkey. The crowd turned eastward en masse.

"That way lies Mecca." Brahim explained.

The ceremony, recitations of the Quran, lasted about an hour. Friends and relatives spoke in Arabic and Berber, each using the language they were most comfortable with. Afterward, the Jews paid their respects to the shepherd and introduced themselves to Charlie.

A young Jewish man in his twenties asked, "Are you American?"

"Yes. Why?"

"I've always wanted to go. I have a cousin in New Jersey."

"What are you doing here?"

"I'm from Israel here on pilgrimage."

An older gentleman spoke up. "For some of us this is our home."

"I thought this was a Muslim country."

"Now we go to the cemetery," interrupted Brahim.

The cart was re-hitched and the procession headed up the dirt road. The only sounds as they climbed were the creaking of the cart and the quiet sobs of the women who trailed the cart from several yards behind.

"Why are the women back there?" Charlie asked.

"This is a very modern Muslim family. Usually it is only the men who go to the cemetery."

Brahim motioned for his silence. They reached an old wrought iron gate.

"Stay here. Only Muslims may enter."

The men unhitched the donkey from the cart. One turned and muttered something to Brahim in Arabic.

"They are asking for you to please watch the donkey."

"My pleasure."

They rolled the cart into the cemetery with Brahim in the group.

Charlie watched the procession until they were lost among the crypts. He stared at the donkey who ignored a fly on his eyelash. The animal smelled earthy and worn. Charlie looked over his shoulder and realized the countryside was green, verdant, abundant with signs of Spring. Some of the city stood out against the mountainside in various hues of blue. A fog was rolling in. This, he realized, was as good a place as any to lie in repose.

The empty cart was rolled out a few minutes later and the donkey was hitched up once again.

The Jews were waiting and other townspeople had arrived and set up tables of food and carafes of warm Moroccan tea.

Charlie was drawn to the Jews and wanted to know their story.

"We are all over Morocco and welcomed," the older man explained. "I am of the Tovashim. My family has lived peacefully among our Muslim brethren since ancient times."

Brahim brought Charlie a plate of food. "The lamb is especially fresh."

"I see you have met the Jews," he said. "Have they told you the legend of the Blue City?"

The elder Jew admonished him in Berber.

"I don't speak Berber very well. Arabic or French, please," Brahim asked.

The old Jew turned to Charlie. "The legend is a fairy tale."

"During and after the Inquisition in Spain, the Jews fled to this country," Brahim began.

"Some of us were already here," insisted the old Jew.

"The new Jews…"

"The Megorashim…"

"They asked if they could stay. Moroccans said they could, but they would have to paint their houses blue to be easily identified," continued Brahim.

"Then came World War Two and the Nazi Desert Rat, Rommel."

"Everyone painted their houses blue to hide the Jews in plain sight."

"A fairy tale!" said the old man.

"You're welcome!" Brahim cried.

The shepherd, his late wife's brother-in-law, and his son approached them. The old Jew and Omar embraced and traded kisses. Omar, his face glistening from recent tears, wrapped Charlie in a warm hug and kissed both cheeks then, through Brahim, introduced his in-laws.

"My wife's brother, Hassan and his son, Mohammed." They,

too, embraced Charlie and Brahim.

"Come," said the old Jew to Charlie. "Walk with me."

The waning moon cast a hazy glow as they strolled away from the light of the funeral feast.

"My name is Isaac. You, too, are Jewish if I'm not mistaken?"

"Charlie Wise. Yes. Yes, I am."

"What's troubling you, Charlie?"

"What do you mean?"

"You seem very nervous, restless. And your hand trembles with a life of its own."

"It's Parkinson's."

"Ah, but there's more!"

"I'm looking for, I don't know…"

"Absolution?" Isaac offered.

"Forgiveness? That's part of it. I want to make amends. As a good Jew, how do I do that? Mitzvah? Or is my fate sealed?"

Isaac shrugged. "You would have to ask the younger ones from Israel. They have all the answers. Me? Our people have been shoulder to shoulder with the Muslims for so many generations, I don't know the difference between hallal and kosher!"

He registered the look on Charlie's face.

"Have I offended you?"

"No, but it doesn't give me hope."

"I'll tell you a secret, Charles. The secret is…" he leaned forward conspiratorially. "Don't be a schmuck. Especially at first when you're trying to make a good impression."

"That's how I always start out. I show them my true self so they're not surprised later."

"Do you think people are inherently good or evil?"

"Do you mean are they born that way? I think we lean one way or the other. From then on, it's a toss-up based on environment and happenstance."

"Did you know Aadil, the shepherd's wife?"

"No."

"She was the most devout woman I ever met. A beautiful woman in her youth. She left the journey from Marrakech to Chefchouen a long time ago to live with her sister here. She hated the time apart from Omar, but she hated the hardscrabble existence that women have on the trail. The women climb the hillsides to round up the sheep who have strayed."

In the distance they saw the casbah lit up for the tourists and heard a donkey's bray on the wind.

"I, too, will die here someday among these gentle people. But no one must ever know that she was my friend."

"Is that some sort of euphemism, Isaac?"

"Don't you dare sully her reputation! Would you deny her Paradise?"

"Calm down! It was just the way you were carrying on…"

"You don't understand the culture, Charles. Just spending time with me one on one…."

"Interesting choice of words."

"Aadil was a good Muslim! She could never give Omar children and it made her sad and lonely. She went to school when she was young and her thirst for knowledge never left her."

We could never have kids. I don't think it ever bothered Margo.

Isaac dug into the pockets of his overcoat, pulling out a sheaf of papers.

"She was a gifted poet. Here!" He shoved a page at Charlie.

"It's in French, I can't read it."

"Ah, yes. You Americans, clinging to one language, the one true God English." Isaac looked down at the page in the faint light, tears gathering in the corners of his eyes. "It's titled, 'One woman.'"

Une femme seule
Son ventre un desert aride.
Sa famille disparue, defaite
Moutons perdus dans le desert.

"It sounds pretty."

"Listen to what it's saying. It speaks to what Aadil felt was the true purpose of women!"

One woman alone
Her womb a barren desert
Her family gone, undone
Lost sheep in the desert.

"Wow. Kinda bleak."
"She felt she had been denied her purpose for living."
Not Margo. One miscarriage, the bad news, and she carried on as though nothing had happened.
And suddenly the floodgates opened.
Charlie leaned against Isaac and the tears surprised him with their volume and ferocity. He could not *not* cry. He felt Aadil's overwhelming sadness as if it was his own. It *was* his own. He cried for the lost opportunity to create a family, the miracle of birth, holding a giggling toddler is his arms, wiping away preschool tears, awkward father/daughter dances, sending her off to college, a bittersweet wedding, the birth of his first grandchild, the whole circle of life as he and Margo forged an unbreakable bond that would carry them through the years. That was what they had lost.
We stopped feeling because it hurt too damn much.

Chapter 14

Five days and sixteen hours was a long time to hang onto the aha! moment of an epiphany. Charlie hadn't called Margo to announce his impending arrival into JFK. He wasn't really sure what he was going to do. It was late by the time he cleared customs so he booked a room at the airport Marriott to plan his next move.

They gave him a room on the third floor by the stairwell. He skipped the elevator and huffed and puffed up to his room.

Man, I'm out of shape. Going down was going to be much easier.

Long flights drained his energy. He was pretty sure sleep would come to him as soon as he lay his head on the pillow.

Obviously, Margo was at the top of his very short list. She had put up with so much from him, *decades* of bullshit. She was a fucking saint.

An hour later he forced himself to get up. His kind of tired wasn't sleepy, it was a weariness that seeped into him. Local time was 10 pm. He hadn't had a drink the whole three weeks he was in Morocco. He didn't really miss alcohol, but it might make him sleep.

He slipped on jeans, a t-shirt and a windbreaker. It was cold outside, but he wasn't going outside, just down the stairs to the bar.

The stairwell was chillier than he thought it would be. He never realized he missed a step until the world seemed to pull away from him and tilt. Hard.

He knew where he was before he opened his eyes. *A hospital.*

His little brother, John, walked in sipping a cup of coffee. "Hey, world traveler. How many cups of coffee am I holding?"

Charlie managed a weak chuckle. "Two."

"Don't you wish! I didn't think you'd be awake yet."

John walked over to the bed and gave his brother an awkward hug. They looked at each other critically, taking stock of the changes since they had last been together. *God he looks old!! I hope I don't look that bad!*

"Man, you look like shit!" He had a lump on the side of his head and his body felt stiff.

"How long have I been here?"

"That's an easy one. Two days."

"Did anybody call Margo?"

"That's the *last* person I would call! I gave her a buzz a couple weeks ago to see how she was doing after her boob job. She hung up on me!"

"Thanks for checking on her."

"Was that sarcasm or were you really thanking me?"

"Nah. Serious. I thought I was ready to talk to her, but maybe not. I don't want her to worry."

"Hey! Doc James was here. No jokes. All serious like. He said Dr. Brain was on her way. Dr. Brain? Was he making that up?"

"She's my neurologist."

Dr. Brain appeared as if summoned, dressed casually in a flowery blouse and slacks and the obligatory white coat.

John was perplexed. "You just fell, right? No Brain injury?"

"She hasn't touched me!"

It took John a moment before he caught the joke. "I'm only laughing because you're injured and I feel sorry for you."

Dr. Brain took a look at his pupils and consulted his chart. "Go ahead. I've heard them all."

"Nah. Too easy," John replied. A look of concern settled into his face. "What's wrong with him, doctor?"

She looked at Charlie. "You haven't told him?"

"I haven't told anybody. Well, that's not exactly true. I told Isaac and Brahim in Morocco, Arthur…"

"Arthur in Texas? You haven't seen him in 30-40 years! You told him before me?"

"Quit making this about you," Charlie said.

"That's right. As usual, it's all about you."

"Hey, I said I was sorry."

"No you didn't," John pointed out.

"Oh. Right. Sorry. If it's any consolation, I haven't told Margo, either."

"You still haven't told me! What the fuck is wrong?"

"I'm dying."

"What?"

Brain interrupted. "That's not completely true." She turned to John. "He's got Parkinson's. He could have ten, twenty years left, at least."

"Tell him what some of the late stages look like," Charlie urged.

Dr. Brain looked exasperated. "Dementia, hallucinations, muscle spasms and pain."

"So, I could check out before I *check out*, get my drift?"

"But she said you've got ten or twenty years."

Charlie looked at the doctor. "We don't really know how slowly or quickly the disease may progress, do we?"

"With that kind of attitude, Mr. Wise, you might as well lie down right here and expire. Your tombstone can say, 'See, I told you I was dying!'"

"I like to think I'm settling my affairs."

"So many affairs!" John snickered.

Oh my God! I forgot about Tina. John doesn't know I did his wife.

"Which brings me to a confession for you."

"I'm all ears."

"Tina and I, a long time ago…"

"I know."

"She told you?"

"I sorta guessed it and she sorta confessed."

"Sorry?" Charlie offered.

"Was that an apology? Because if it was, it sucked."

"I apologize. Sincerely."

"And you'll never do it again?"

"I couldn't even if I wanted to." He gestured to his crotch. "Nothing's happening."

"So, if your peepee worked you would still be the Charlie Wise everybody loves to hate, right?"

"Well, there's the dying thing…"

"Jesus, Charlie. You're Mr. Worst Case Scenario. I think you'll be around to torture your loved ones long after I'm gone."

"That's the thing, John. What if I'm not? If I live another few years, won't they be better ones for everybody concerned if I go on my apology tour now?"

"What do you think, Doctor?"

"I think if Charlie can walk now without getting light-headed or dizzy, he should check out and go home. Hold off on the tour for a couple days. Use a cane. I'll see you later."

"Can you give me a ride back to the Marriott?" he asked his brother.

"You're checked out. Your shit's at my house."

"I'm not ready to see Margo. Especially like this."

"You can sleep on my couch for a couple days, but don't even *look* at Tina!"

"Do you mind swinging by Harvey's first?"

Chapter 15

Charlie hadn't visited his agent at his office for a long time, the phone was so much faster and cheaper than the price of gas and parking. The third story cubbyhole seemed more littered with galleys and correspondence than he had ever seen it. Harvey was a scrawny, bald man inching his way through his seventies? Eighties? He still maintained appearances, showing up for work every day in a suit and tie, ready to conduct business. His voice was raspy from decades of Pall Malls and a love of Cuban cigars.

He studied Charlie for a moment behind dirty bifocals. "Long time, no hear."

"I've been traveling, trying to clear my head."

"Did it work?"

"You tell me."

"Ready to write that book? Tell me a story."

"A guy's dying…"

Harvey gave him a raspberry. "It's been done. Next."

"Wait, you didn't even give me a chance to expound…"

"The public's not buying tear-jerkers right now."

"So, no sappy dialogue, sentimental scenes, that kind of crap?"

"Right. Without those ingredients it's not a tear-jerker. It's the opposite."

"Nobody's laughing if that's what you mean."

"Is there sex?" asked Harvey, ticking off invisible boxes.

"Oh yeah."

"Blood?"

"Does it sell?"

"Oh yeah."

"Okay, it's in there, but just a little because it makes me queasy."

"What's your hook?"

"It's me," said Charlie.

"First person then? That could work."

"No. It's *me* dying."

He looked Charlie in the eye for a moment. "Really?"

"Really."

"Then what the fuck are you doing here? Go enjoy your life, what's left of it."

"I really wanted to leave something behind to say, 'Charlie Wise was here.'"

"Spray paint your name on the Statue of Liberty."

"I wanted to leave something for the ages, a real legacy. Like *Tom Sawyer* or *The Great Gatsby*."

"Do you realize the chances of your book getting published, being recognized and praised by the critics, and lasting on the library shelf for a hundred years is slim to none?"

"I'm dead serious. I want to do this."

"*Dead Serious.* Great title. Here's the book you're going to write: I'm dying and this is what I'm going to do to leave my mark. Put sex in there, like we agreed. Are we talking the Great American novel or something hot and torrid?"

"For a minute I thought you were going to suggest my story."

"Look, do you want to write a gut-wrenching saga with a downer ending with your protagonist alone on the beach as he walks into the ocean never to be seen again? Or an entertaining romp that will sell thousands of books and be forgotten in a month?"

"What am I going to do with all that money? I'll be dead."

"You're right, Charlie. Don't think about Margo or me and my kids. Be selfish. Write the book you were meant to write. Spill your soul on the page."

"I know you're pissed, but I have to do this, Harvey."

"Nah, I understand." He pulled a book from the tall bookcase behind him and handed it to Charlie.

"*How to Write a Novel in 30 Days.*"

"You're going to need it. Go. Check in once in a while so I'll know you're not dead yet."

Chapter 16

The living room had a bigger TV. There were more knickknacks on the shelves.

"So, have you talked to Margo?" John asked.

Tina walked out of the kitchen drying her hands. She looked ageless, her auburn hair coiffed perfectly. "Dinner's ready, boys. How's Margo, Charlie?"

"I don't know. I haven't talked to her. I'm not ready to talk to her yet. I just need a little more time. If you want to know how she's doing, call her. I'm sure she'd love to hear from you two."

"We'll talk over dinner," Tina insisted. "Let's eat."

Tina had roasted the flavor out of a cut of corned beef. It was dry and chewy.

"If you think this is going to get me out of the house sooner, you may be on to something."

"Watch it, buster. We waited dinner on you."

"I'm sorry, I don't walk as fast as I used to."

"Stop it with the attempted Jewish guilt. How long have you had Parkie's, a week?"

"I was diagnosed with *Parkinson's Disease* about three months ago and the progression of the disease is different for each patient. I could be gone tomorrow."

"That's one way to get you out of the house."

"Listen," Charlie said, turning serious. "I have a really big favor to ask."

"No betting money," John said.

"I haven't been to a casino or racetrack in months. No, it's bigger."

"You now have our full attention," said Tina.

"Let me write my novel here."

"How long is that going to take?"

He showed them the book, *How to Write a Novel in 30 Days*. "The book says a month. I'm shooting for three weeks."

Tina and John exchanged glances.

"I'll leave the room so you can discuss it." Charlie told them.

He headed for his brother's home office. *If I'm already writing when they find me, they can't say no.* The computer was password protected. He tried Tina and her birthday and he was in.

As soon as the loud voices stopped in the other room, he was expecting them. Tina had a look like she'd been sucking lemons.

"Three weeks, that's it. First day we don't see you writing, you're out of here." She looked over his shoulder at the screen. "Naming your characters after us isn't going to help extend your stay."

"That wasn't my intention. It's out of gratitude."

"You're full of shit, Charlie."

"So I've been told."

He turned back to the computer and ignored their exit.

Chapter 17

Charlie left the computer for meals and the bathroom, and little else. He would wake every morning and try to hobble up and down the street to shake out the advancing stiffness in his legs. The ritual helped him gather his thoughts about dialogue, structure and plot. John gave him free rein on his desktop and used his phone to catch up on his own emails and conduct company business.

"Got a minute?" John asked a week later.

"Sure." Charlie was happy for a temporary reprieve. He had painted his main character into a corner.

"I have to go to Albany for two days. Are you going to be alright?" He jerked his head toward the kitchen where Tina was making dinner.

"Do you mean am I going to ravage your wife as soon as you're out the door?"

"Well, yeah. By the way, I'm proud of how you're sticking to this writing project. Does it take your mind off your problems?"

"Did you forget what I said about my numb nuts, numb nuts?"

"I just figured you were trying to keep me from worrying."

"Apparently that didn't work. And no, it keeps my mind *on* my problems. That's what I'm writing about."

"Well, focus on those masochistic tendencies and leave my wife alone while I'm gone."

"I'm sorry, did you say lead your wife along while you're gone?"

"Asshole. See you Thursday."

It was raining heavily when Charlie heard John leave.

Tina stuck her head in the door. "Hi. I'm just ordering a pizza tonight, okay?"

Charlie glanced at his watch. "Why is he leaving at rush hour?"

"He said he wanted to get a good night's sleep before his meeting in the morning with his corporate overlords. He's taking his young secretary out to dinner and a schtup."

"I'm sorry, Tina. I had no idea."

"Who do you think taught him that it's okay to cheat on your spouse?"

"Don't put that on me. I believe you were a consenting adult at the time."

"You know what? Fuck the pizza. I'm going to get drunk!"

Uh oh.

"Leave me alone then, will you? I'm in the zone."

"You're going to let a girl drink alone?"

"I believe that's how we got into trouble last time."

She had a naughty grin. "Oh yeah."

"Have fun." He pushed her out the door, closed it behind her and locked it.

During the next two hours Charlie heard glass break, tiny tentative taps at the office door that turned into pounding and a final frustrated curse, an hour of loud TV, then silence.

He opened the door a crack and saw shoes and a dress in the hallway leading to the living room. He heard a low rumbling snore and found her passed out on the sofa in her underwear. He covered her in a blanket and almost stepped on a shattered wine glass as he entered the kitchen. He picked up the shards of glass with the hand vac, wiped up the spilled red wine and wondered where he should sleep.

Sunlight streaming into the office window woke him up. He watched dust motes dance in the air for a minute before he raised his head from the desk. Tina tapped on the door and walked in with a cup of coffee. She was dressed for work.

"Thanks for being such a gentleman last night, you bastard."

"Revenge sex only feels good while you're doing it." Neither remarked on the fact that he couldn't have risen to the occasion anyway.

Tina's cellphone buzzed. "Well well." Sha handed the phone to Charlie.

"It's for you."

Margo. He answered it.

"Hi, Charlie."

"Hi, Margo. How are you?"

"When are you coming home?"

"I asked, how are you."

"You don't really care, Charlie. Don't pretend to care. Do you still live here or should I donate your stuff to Goodwill?"

"Why are you calling?"

"Tina called me last night. She was shit-faced. She asked if it was okay to fuck you."

"What did you... I hope you told her I was off limits."

"I hung up on her."

Good enough.

She turned her attention back to Charlie. "So, what's going on with you? I mean, you've adjusted to life at arm's length with me, we have a comfortable situation here, don't we?"

"Cozy."

"Is it the boob job? Are you still upset about that?"

"Honey, they were fine before. Beautiful...."

"You should see them now. They point straight ahead. They're prettier now than they have ever been."

"You know how much I like big ones, *your* big ones. Can you get some with helium? They'll be bigger, but lighter!"

"You like them so much, Charlie, *you* get them!"

The call was over. Charlie was sure of it.

His phone dinged. It was a topless selfie from Margo. He had to admit. *Those do look pretty good.*

He knew now her operation was not the real issue. He still didn't like the results as much as the before picture he kept in his phone, but he was going to focus on what had been eating at them since that winter morning in 1986.

He felt a flood of emotions wash over him. *Time to sit and write.*

Chapter 18

They went to dinner at Guido's, like in the old days. She glanced around.

"Uh oh. We're going down Memory Lane." She studied his face. "Gambling again, Charlie? How much do you need?"

He felt the old anger rising in him, a half-remembered reflex. She could do that to him, fire up such passion.

"No. I'm here because I want to apologize for being an asshole all those years."

"Why now?"

"I know. I waited too long. But I want to patch up things between us. We're not getting any younger."

"You're a piece of cake, you know that? Every couple of years you start to feel guilty for being such a horrible husband. It just never happens after a trifecta win. And you usually ask for $250: not too much but enough to make a sizable bet in the near future."

"That's always pissed me off about you, Margo. You *think* you know what I'm thinking, but you're so far off, it makes us both mad."

She slid out of the booth and gave him the finger. "Leopards don't change their spots, Charlie. I'm outta here and don't try to stop me."

"Wait!" She was gone. His hand started to shake. He grabbed a pill from his pocket, determined to ride out his off time by faking normal.

He showed up on John and Tina's front stoop, not sure if he should ring the doorbell or just walk in. John opened the door and stood aside.

"Coming in to gather your stuff because you're headed home, I hope?"

"That woman makes my blood pressure shoot through the ceiling," he told John.

"I think you said that the day you met her."

"Yeah, but back then, it wasn't likely to give me a stroke."

"By the way, did you take your meds?" asked John.

"When is Scott coming home for Spring Break? I need a bong hit. Or two. Or three."

"Get it yourself. If you're popped it's like a jaywalking ticket now."

"Nah. I'm getting dizzy all by myself."

"Think of all the money you're saving!"

Tina handed Charlie his pills and a glass of water. He tossed the meds into his mouth and took a big swig of water to gulp them down. "Thanks."

"If anybody needs me, I'll be writing." Pain in his hips and the base of his spine was an everyday thing; it made him lean to the right, bringing on the political jokes. He tried to close the door gently, but it got away from him and made much more noise than he had intended.

Tina looked at John with concern. "Maybe you shouldn't make so many jokes about his Parkinson's."

"Are you kidding? He hides his fear behind the humor."

"He's not laughing."

Chapter 19

"This isn't a piece of shit!"

"Thanks." Charlie knew that was high praise from Harvey. He was marveling at the first five chapters. "So much sex!"

"Uh, thanks?"

"All real?"

Sell the myth. "I don't fuck and tell. Oops."

"And the blood?"

"Coming." *Sooner than later, probably.*

"Get back to work, kiddo. Don't let me hold you up!"

He looked Charlie in the eye. "How ya doing?"

"I have my good days and my bad months."

"Better get cranking, then!"

"Thanks, Harvey. For a minute there, I thought you cared."

"There ain't no legacy if it's not finished. That's what you wanted, right?"

They stared at each other, two grown men grasping the truth of all that was unsaid and reacting with silent stoicism.

"On point. Thanks."

Chapter 20

A week later John and Tina confronted Charlie over dinner. "We know you've been keeping some late hours on your book. That's why we gave you an extra week, but…"

"When are you going to call Margo?" Tina asked.

"She knows where I am. My cell number didn't change."

"Look," she said. "Peggy went home last week. Margo's all healed…"

"Downright perky!" John ventured.

Tina frowned.

"I'm getting to a really critical part of the book. Give me three more days and I'll call her. I promise. The next few pages will tie it all up for her and maybe give us both some closure."

"Three days." Tina challenged.

"Three days."

The next morning, Charlie hovered over breakfast, avoiding the last scene, prolonging the inevitable. *It's the end of everything, the book, my stay away, my life.*

Chapter 21

Harvey was seated at his desk in anticipation. He stretched his arms across the desk.

"Gimme, gimme."

Charlie sat directly across and watched Harvey's face for clues. *Does he like it? Is it still not a piece of shit?*

Harvey read the last page and sat staring off in the distance then turned to Charlie.

"Where's the blood?"

"I was afraid you would say that," Charlie said as he pulled out a .38 and put it in his mouth.

"Oh, Jesus! Don't do that to me!" he screamed at Charlie.

"You didn't like that ending?" Charlie smirked.

"No. Too real. Back it off a bit."

"Still want some blood?"

"No. That was enough for me."

"So, I can do this my way?"

"Ah, you're not talking about tears and all the maudlin shit?"

"I don't know. The ending hasn't been written yet."

"All right. Get out of here. But hurry back with something good and saleable!"

Chapter 22

Dr. Brain ran Charlie through the manual dexterity tests without comment.

"So, how was your trip to Thailand?"

"Fine, but that was months ago."

"I thought that was Morocco."

"I went there, too, but after Thailand."

"I'm glad to see your memory's working. I see you're still using the cane. How is your balance? Any dizziness?"

"Fine and a little."

"Are you sure you're not having any balance issues and you're just using the cane as a crutch?"

"So you do have a sense of humor!"

"I'm sure it's no match for yours. Any pain?" she asked as he winced getting off the examination table.

"Some. Muscle spasms in my legs and lower back problems."

"Pain on a scale of one to ten?"

"Eight to eleven."

"Smoke pot. Unless you want some opioids?" she asked.

"None of the pills. I'm already up to ten pills a day with my current meds. I heard pot doesn't do anything for the pain."

"True, but you forget you're hurting." She locked eyes with him, serious. "How are you otherwise? Depressed?"

If I tell her about Thailand, she'll either have me locked up for observation or give me happy pills. "It comes and goes."

"I can get you into a support group."

"Nah. Group's not my thing. I always try to take over the

meeting. It's an old habit from my ad agency days. You know, battle of the ideas."

She handed him a card. "If things get too bad, give these guys a call or 9-1-1."

He could just imagine his neighbors freaking out at the sight of an ambulance, the stares and polite questions.

"Thanks, Doc."

"Chin up, Charlie. No matter how bad you've got it, somebody's got it worse."

Chapter 23

He came to the breakfast table and threw down his finished manuscript. "I owe you for three reams of paper."

Tina looked up and asked, "Can we read it?"

"I was hoping you would. Today."

John picked it up and hefted the package. "There's got to be 300 pages here."

"Two hundred, eighty-seven. I know you can't read it in a single day, but Tina can."

"I'd better get started," she said.

She plopped into the recliner in the living room. At noon, they ordered pizza.

Tina glanced up and said, "You're an asshole, Charlie."

They cleaned up the empty beer bottles, the paper plates, and the pizza box as Tina read on.

Charlie watched emotions flit across her face as she encountered critical passages in the story. The cuckoo clock on the wall seemed inordinately loud. Suddenly, Tina gasped.

A few minutes later, a couple of tears rolled down her cheeks, unheeded. She seemed to notice that the room had grown darker as they moved into evening. She leaned over and turned on a table lamp.

"Almost done."

Charlie busied himself setting the dinner table as John wrestled with chicken on the stove. Tina walked in thumping the manuscript.

"This is fucking good."

"How good?" he asked, uncertain he wanted to know.

"Call Margo."

Chapter 24

She picked up on the first ring.

"Your shit's gone. You took too long to get back to me."

Before he gave himself a chance to bristle, he answered, "No biggie. I'd like to talk to you. Can we try dinner again?"

"Tina tells me you're not gambling."

"Nope."

He waded into the silence. "I wrote a book."

"I heard." *Damn, Tina. Upstaging him left and right.*

"I'd like you to read it."

"I'm pretty busy…"

"I know you don't like to read. How about I read it to you?"

"I like to read; I'm just not interested in the stuff you write about. Let's not do Guido's again. I'll make us something."

"I'll bring the book."

"Okay."

He turned around to confront Tina and John. "Save the high fives for tomorrow night."

He stared at his own front door. *Should I knock or walk in like I own the place? Because I do.* She hid behind the door as she opened it for him. She had Bocelli on the stereo. She either had forgotten how much he hated Bocelli or was messing with him.

Charlie looked around the room to see how much had changed and discovered, contrary to what she had told him, she hadn't touched any of his things. The broken miniature Chichén Itzá that came from the previous house that was missing a staircase still sat next to one of her sad Hummel clowns.

He smelled the beef enchiladas, his favorite food, period. He turned to greet her. She was wearing something with a plunging neckline. They awkwardly fumbled a platonic kiss that just missed his ear.

"Hi."

"Hi," she replied.

He looked at her chest. "They *are* perky."

"For that kind of money they'd better be."

"You look good."

She took in his jeans, Hawaiian shirt, sport coat. "So do you."

"Smells good."

"Me or the enchiladas?"

"B… you, of course! Though I do love Mexican food."

She gave him a tight-lipped skeptical smile. "Dinner will be ready soon."

Charlie took that as a sign to plop down on the sofa.

"I know you prefer beer with your enchiladas, but would you like to have a glass of wine with me?"

"Sure."

Margo came back from the kitchen carrying two Coronas. "Just kidding. *Salud.*"

"Remember that sultry, sweaty night in Cabo?" she asked.

Okay, kids. Time for a pop quiz.

"You mean our honeymoon? Of course."

"We would have sold our souls for an ice-cold beer that night."

"And you don't even like beer!"

"There's a time for it: then and now!"

The oven dinged from the other room. "Have a seat at the table. I'll be right back."

He considered his regular spot at the head of the table and picked a more neutral position directly across from her. He dragged his place setting to the new location. He jumped up to help as she emerged from the kitchen with steaming enchiladas. She saw he had moved his plate across from hers.

"Doesn't this feel like a first date?" she asked.

"Do you mean because we're both on our best behavior? Don't get me wrong, I like it."

"I think we both just want this night to go right."

Charlie took in a forkful of enchilada, cheese dripping. "I have something important to tell you," he said.

"I want a divorce."

He felt like she had punched him in the stomach.

"Couldn't you have waited till dessert?"

"I have waited a long time for this!"

"Would 15 minutes have mattered?"

"I have some papers for you to sign."

Charlie sighed. "Go get them. I'm feeling generous tonight."

She returned immediately with the divorce papers and lay them out before him.

Charlie found a pen in his sport coat.

"It's not going to matter anyhow."

"Why is that, Charlie?"

"I'll be dead soon."

"Is this some kind of pity move for the house?"

"No, Margo. I mean it. I'm dying."

"What's wrong?"

"I've got Parkinson's."

"Do you mean that thing that Michael J. Fox has?"

"Yeah. You will understand better after you read this," he said as he pulled his draft from a briefcase.

"So, you finally did it."

"I'm hoping after you read it, we can talk."

"Well, you're about ten years too late. Did you think all would be forgiven and you could come home? You've been gone three months! That's called abandonment."

"I don't know, but if you just read…"

"Date's over, Charlie. I need some alone time. I have to think."

"You know, I was going to offer to do the dishes."

"I've been able to afford a maid with you gone. She comes twice a week."

"Goodnight, Margo. I'll call you tomorrow."

"Better give me the whole weekend. I don't read as fast as Tina."

"Aha!"

"I'm also not Tina. I'm at the end of a very long rope with you."

"Understood." He opened the door. "I love you, Margo."

No response. He didn't wait for one.

Where to now? He really didn't feel like going back to John and Tina's and going through the third degree. He had the taxi drop him off at a hotel around the corner from their townhouse.

His hand was shaking and he remembered it was way past time to take his afternoon dose of meds.

Charlie's cell phone rang. It was Tina.

"Well? How'd it go?"

"C'mon, Tina. I'm sure you've already got the scoop from Margo."

"Nope. Bitch wouldn't spill the beans."

"She knew about the book. She knew about the Parkinson's, but didn't seem concerned about it."

"I told her you were looking for sympathy, acting like you were going to wake up dead one of these days."

"Thanks. That was my ace."

"Nah. The book is your ace."

"Margo doesn't like to read. She'll give up 10 pages in."

"It's about her. Granted, it's mostly about you. She'll keep reading," Tina assured him.

"I'm going to go now. It's been a long night."

"Bullshit. What is it, nine-thirty? It's still early. Come over for a nightcap."

"I don't look good in hats."

"Haha. John's got some 18-year-old Scotch he's been saving for a special occasion or a rainy day, I forget which. Come help him drink it."

She could be relentless. Fucking realtors. "Fine. On my way."

They both answered the door and searched his face for a clue on how he was taking this.

John hoisted the bottle of Scotch and a glass. "Rocks? Straight up?"

"One cube of ice. A couple drops of water to bring out the flavor."

"That's right. You and Margo brought this back from Scotland."

"She wants a divorce," Charlie said.

"Don't be silly," Tina assured him. "You'll be between the sheets by Sunday night."

Charlie sniffed the amber liquid and took a slow sip to savor the taste. It brought back memories. He and Margo had run out onto the golf course, stripped naked and ran between the sprinklers.

"Too many fucking sheep," he said.

"What?"

"Scotland. Three sheep for every one person. Of course, some guys like those kinds of odds."

"Eww," said Tina.

"Lots of history," John offered.

"We went to this beautiful castle by the sea. It was drizzling and Margo whipped out the umbrella she had brought along on our trip. There she was, standing by the drab brown ramparts and the cannons, all the trees dark sticks, winter-bare, and she was posing with this bright, multi-colored umbrella, like a rainbow after the storm."

"Another dram?" John asked.

"Sure." The Scotch tasted of currants and smoke. It was warm and soothing as it went down. He thought of the distillery they had visited on an afternoon. They were closing at two, but the owner happened by and gave them the grand tour.

They sat by the fire as Charlie recalled stories from his and Margo's trip to Scotland; he and John drained the bottle.

Tina wandered into the room in a robe. "I'm going to bed, boys. Charlie, want the couch?"

He glanced at his watch and was startled to see it was just shy of midnight. "No thanks, guys. It's not far and I have to take my meds."

Chapter 25

The morning was bright with a chilly hint of autumn surrendering to winter. He walked the four blocks back to John and Tina's where they were just getting up.

Tina insisted on making them scrambled eggs and toast. "The book is great. I loved that part at the Moroccan funeral," John said.

"I'm impressed. You actually read the book."

"Actually, that's as far as I got."

"It moved me, Charlie. And it will move Margo," Tina said.

"That would be nice, but I'm just trying to show her who I was and who I want to be and, of course, apologize and spend my last days with her."

"That could be several years, Charlie. I talked with a friend of mine who works for a neurologist and she said the progression of the disease is very slow. She said you could very well have a regular 80 plus years like the rest of us."

"Thanks, Tina. My new motto is, "Hope for the best and plan for the worst.""

"Very practical."

"I think you downplayed it a little too much with Margo. When I tried to bring it up last night, she pretty much ignored me." He shot her a dirty look. *Like it was no big deal.*

His phone rang. It was Randy.

"Thank God it's you! I've been trying to call you back to apologize."

"Yeah, I know. I saw the 42 missed calls and heard the seven voicemails. How about a *cock*tail after work?"

"You're incorrigible, you know that?"

"That's why you love me!"

The bar Randy picked was near their old stomping grounds near Times Square. He wasn't fond of the new cleaned-up Square. Tourist families wandering around staring at the electronic billboards, taking photos with the Hulk or Minnie Mouse for a buck, openly gawking at the Naked Cowboy who wasn't really naked, decked out in cowboy hat, cowboy boots, and a pair of tighty-whities. After dark, wilder tourists brought back some of the seamy side of the old Times Square, dry-humping the Cowboy and sharing it on Instagram.

Charlie walked into the Pig n Whistle and looked for either Randy or a booth. Randy had already found them one.

"Yoo-hoo, Charlie! Over here!' he yelled loud enough that he got everyone's attention. Randy was loud even for New York.

He threw his arms around Charlie and gave him a prolonged hug. He then kissed Charlie on the lips. *How am I supposed to take that? What do I do?*

"Sorry, Charlie. I'm just fucking with you."

"No problem." *My body didn't respond. I guess I'm straight. Good to know.*

"Wow, Charlie! I'm impressed. I kissed you and you didn't deck me!"

"I just came back from Morocco. Guys kiss and hold hands, but it's not a gay thing."

"How do you know? I hear if they come out, they're dead."

"So, I really wanted to make peace with you, Randy, because we've been friends for a long, long time. Though I didn't think about your gayness until you told us on that camping trip five years ago."

"I was born this way, Charlie."

"Yeah, I know, Randy. You told me."

He reached across the table and took hold of Randy's hand. The waiter finally arrived.

"Are you gents ready to order or I can come back…"

"Just a couple of pints," Charlie growled.

He turned back to Randy. "I'm holding your hand because I have something important to tell you. That I tried to tell you when I called that day, but you freaked out on me…"

"Sorry. Now are you going to hold my hand all night or tell me what's up with you?"

"I've got Parkinson's Disease."

"Shit. I'm sorry to hear that. My uncle had it. He died."

"How old was he?"

"85."

"You know, then, that it can take you at any time."

"Yeah, but…"

"You would probably agree with me that there's no time like the present to get my affairs in order."

"Charlie, are you selling life insurance?"

"Please don't make fun of me, Randy. I would never do that to you." Randy rolled his eyes.

"How can I help you?"

"I need to make it right by you."

"You want to make it right by me?" Charlie nodded eagerly. "I'm taking you to another bar."

It was called Big Apple Ranch. Charlie was surprised to hear country music in the middle of Manhattan and, as his eyes adjusted, to see so many guys do-si-doing together. There were cowboy hats and cowboy boots, little guys and big, burly men and even straight couples and everyone was having a great time.

They had a drink and then another. While the band took a break, a DJ took over. A blonde with too much makeup asked him to dance. It was a slow romantic oldie. She pulled him up tight and put her head on his chest.

She lifted her head and gave him a long, sloppy kiss. Randy walked up to him on the dance floor.

"Thought you might like to know, Hayden is trans."

Charlie's hand confirmed it. "Come on," Hayden said. "I'll buy you a beer."

The three of them found a table. Hayden smiled at Charlie. "Go ahead. Ask me anything."

For the next half hour, Charlie asked and Hayden answered. She had transitioned about six months before and was still adjusting to the hormones, but yes, she had always felt she was a woman inside. Yes, she still liked football and, he was surprised to learn, still preferred sex with women.

"Were there any problems?"

"I was 15 when I came out and my parents went ballistic. I was kicked out of the family and the house."

"Tell me honestly, were you born this way or were you just kind of lazy and there were only boys around?"

"Jeez, Randy. How do you stay friends with this guy?"

"Pay attention, Charlie. Which is easier: If you could have sex where your dad winks and pats you on the back or pretend sex doesn't interest you when all your hormones are firing at once?" asked Hayden.

"Act on the impulse to be your true self just once and you're either scarred for life or maybe dead." Charlie mused. "You know, I'm not feeling nearly as buzzed as I should be by now."

"Is that your way of saying you understand?"

"Definitely not! I understand lust. Human nature. I understand the male sex drive. Any time, anywhere. But trying to understand a woman is frustrating, sexy, baffling, but ultimately rewarding… until you find out you were all wrong."

Randy wandered in during the discussion to see how the education of Charlie Wise was progressing and had to admit his old friend had come a long way.

"Hey, Randy," he asked. "If I kiss you, does that mean I'm gay or just experimenting?"

"In your case, Charlie, it means you've had too much to drink."

Charlie suddenly look serious and stared his friend in the eye.

"I'm dying, Randy."

"We all are, honey. Some just a little faster than others."

"Yeah but, I've got an expiration stamp on my forehead."

"Charlie, how long have we been friends?"

About 35 years."

"No, really."

"About ten minutes."

"Very good. Here's a question: if your best friend is gay, are you gay, too?"

Charlie thought for a moment. "It could mean I didn't realize it, because you were secretly communicating with the gay part of me, a part of me just lying there, waiting for me to awaken to my gayness or like some subliminal message slowly turning me gay."

"Sounds pretty stupid to me."

Charlie turned to Randy. "Am I still irresistible?"

"Around closing time, yes."

"I can promise you one thing, Charlie. Nothing will ever happen that you don't want to happen," Hayden chimed in.

"Good to know."

"That also means you can't fake a blackout the next day," Randy explained.

"I know we got off the main subject, but I need you to hear me."

"I know. You're dying."

"Yeah. Parkinson's."

"Who's the celebrity spokesperson for this one? Oh yeah, Michael J. Fox. Did you guys meet and swap surgery stories?"

"You know, I'm not drunk enough not to figure out what you're doing."

"What's that, Charlie?"

"You're saying everybody has some little something that people pick at like a scar. And they'll pick at it and pick at it, till everybody notices it. That's your gayness and my Parkinson's tremor."

All the while we're acting weirder and weirder, trying to pretend we're as "normal" as everybody else.

"And what is the proper response, Charlie?"

"You say, 'Fuck 'em!'"

"And what would you say about coming back to my place?"

"Fuck you. Uber's on the way."

"Ouch!"

"I learned a lot, guys," Charlie confessed. He looked at Hayden and mouthed *Sorry!* in her direction.

"Thank you!"

She came over and gave him another wet sloppy kiss.

"Good luck with Margo."

Charlie left, headed for the hotel. He felt a little light-headed. Was it the booze or the disease? It was getting harder to determine the difference.

Chapter 26

Charlie woke on Sunday morning and sighed. He missed the old routine with Margo of coffee in their special mugs, the Sunday *Times* and bacon and eggs.

His phone rang. It was Margo.

"I woke up thinking about our Sunday breakfasts. Would you like to come over?"

"I'll be right there." He felt optimistic enough to check out of his hotel room.

He was at her doorstep fifteen minutes later with a box of doughnuts under one arm and his suitcase on wheels trailing behind.

She opened the door, her face betraying no emotion. "Come in. Let's talk."

He noticed that, unlike other Sunday mornings, Margo was not lounging around in her pajamas. She was dressed professionally. She responded to the questioning look he gave her. "I'm selling real estate."

His response was a nonjudgmental "hmm," but she took the monosyllable for reproach.

"It keeps me busy and I meet all sorts of interesting people."

"I'm glad you're happy."

"It was a beautiful book, Charlie."

He was tempted to test her recollections of important events in the book, but only one really meant anything to him. He saw this small test as a fork in the road of their relationship.

"Does anything in the book really stick out for you?"

"I'm not sure what you…"

"Don't you see, Margo? Don't you see that the loss of the baby sent us spiraling off in different directions?" He noticed the tears in her eyes.

"Yes! Yes, I did! But you were so cold. You said, 'Thank, God, it wasn't a baby yet.' At that moment I hated you."

"But you never said anything. You acted like it was no big deal!"

"That's when the walls went up. I wasn't going to break down in front of you because I knew I couldn't count on you to be there for me."

"Margo, I'm here now. I was hurting then, too, but I was supposed to be a rock for you." He reached out for her and pulled her into his arms. "I am so sorry, honey. I've been a shitty husband."

"Yes, you have. And maybe you will be still." She pulled away. Charlie could feel the walls coming back up.

"I'm asking for another chance. Please."

"Because you're dying."

"My eyes are open now. Maybe that's because this diagnosis opened them for me. I've got some perspective now."

"And you can't get it up so now you're safe. Or is it just me?"

Man, that hurt. "No, it's not just you. I can't even get it up for me."

"That's karma."

"Margo, I've been a fool. The difference is we both know it now."

"What do you want, Charlie? Do you want me to take you back? Because I'm not sure I'm ready to do that."

Hello, Marriott? I'm coming home.

"Here's what I want: I want you to trust me. Again. I know I'll need to rebuild that trust. I want to find a way to make up for all the times, all the ways, I've hurt you. And if that eventually leads to us living together again as man and wife, I would like that, too."

"It's not happening today, Charlie. Understand?"

"Yeah, I get that. Can you at least tell me divorce is off the table for now?"

"Thank you for sharing your epiphany. And a beautiful book. I'm sorry about your diagnosis. But I don't know if you're really a changed man or just a desperate one. Let's just take it a day at a time. When we both feel we've reached a level of comfort with each other…"

"Do you mean a stage where neither one of us is walking on eggshells, worried we might accidentally say the wrong thing?"

"Exactly."

"That would be nice." *Because I've been doing it for the last thirty years.*

Margo seemed to finally notice the suitcase he had left by the door. "Hoping for a better outcome? Do you need a change of clothes?"

"Nah. I've been keeping up on my laundry at John and Tina's. And, yeah, I was full of hope when I got here."

She pecked him on the cheek. "Give it time, Charlie."

"I don't know how much of that I have, honey."

"I promise I'll consider that in my future decisions."

They were at the door. He tried to embrace her, but she backed away.

"Take care of yourself, Charlie."

"Okay."

He met her eyes as she closed the door, then turned to leave. He fell sideways into the rose bushes.

The door flew open and Margo held out a hand to help him up.

"What are you doing in the rose bushes?"

"I'm searching for something witty to say, but I'm in too much pain."

In a moment he was standing next to her as they dusted him off. She surveyed his scratches. "You look like you were in a cat fight and the cat won." She turned serious. "Are you okay?"

"More embarrassed than hurt. Fucking Parkinson's. I suppose I should eventually consider using a cane."

"This is Parkinson's?"

"Yeah. Dizziness, lightheadedness. Remember when we tried

that new ride at the amusement park and I had vertigo for a week? That was an early sign."

"Look. You're shaking."

"That's my tremor. I'm late on my meds. That's probably why I fell."

She brought a glass of water and he gulped down his pills.

"Thanks for the assist. I'll be leaving. Again."

"Are you sure you're okay?"

"As good as it's going to get. Unless I win the lottery or you take me back."

"Are you sure this wasn't a move for sympathy?"

"We may never know. I almost forgot: Can I trouble you for the book printout? I'm going to see Harvey and I don't have access to a printer."

"Can't he just read it off the computer screen? I thought this was my very own copy."

"You know Harvey. Old-fashioned. Loves to dog-ear the pages for later reference."

She retrieved the book and reluctantly handed it over.

"Don't worry. I'll get you your very own copy once it's printed. I'll sign it, even. It'll have that new-book smell that you like."

"Okay. It really is a wonderful book. I laughed and I cried. Some bits were a little too close to real life, but it's fiction, isn't it?

"Yes, it is."

"Good. I would hate to think the hero, John, was really going to die of his disease."

"Yes, that would be tragic. Well, I will talk to you soon." He landed a quick peck on the cheek this time.

"Give my best to Harvey."

He nodded and closed the door before she could reach it. He realized his body ached from the tumble and it was going to be a long tortuous hike to the subway station.

Chapter 27

"Is this the *real* last few pages?"

"Yep. You're not the first person to read it all the way through, though."

"Another agent?"

"No."

"Then it's cool. What did Margo think of it?"

"She liked it, I guess."

"Hmm. You guess? Not a good sign."

"It was personal. No offense, but why does it matter what she thought?"

"She's your audience. You should ask yourself, 'Who am I writing this for?' before you write word one."

"She *was* who I was writing this for. More than anyone, I wanted her understanding and forgiveness."

"Then where did you go wrong?"

"Well, it's like this: the first time I saw E.T., the Extra Terrestrial, I felt my emotions were being manipulated. I wanted to do that, but with a little more finesse."

"You were going for the tear-jerker, right?"

"I was going for sympathy. How do you get that without pulling a few tears out of your reader?"

"That, Charlie, is the secret to great writing. If you can do that, you've got a hit."

"Shit, I thought I was done with this thing."

"Go home…" Charlie gave him a look. "I mean go to the hotel and give it a read-through. Maybe something will come to you."

Charlie looked dejected. "Maybe you'll find that crucial scene that hangs it all together," offered Harvey.

"One more shot then I give up."

Chapter 26

Tina and John were expecting him. "Harvey called." John offered his laptop.

"My laptop will ensure you have complete peace and quiet," John said.

Tina handed him the thumb drive.

"The whole book is on here." Tina pecked him on the cheek.

"Just don't forget to eat regularly. I hear they have 24-hour room service."

He turned to leave and felt frozen to the spot, his legs refusing to cooperate. Then the moment passed and he headed down the street, with the laptop in a side pocket of his bag on wheels, manuscript under his arm, to his home-away-from-home. He considered taking a cab four blocks, but after all that had happened, he preferred to breathe in Spring and go over the story in his mind.

He walked, deep in thought. The evening had grown chilly and he fished his coat out of his bag.

"Hey, buddy! Hey!" Someone was coming up from behind, moving faster than Charlie that was possible. The guy was drunk or stoned or both, *something* that made him unpredictable and maybe dangerous.

Ignore him. Maybe he'll go away. He had grown up in the area and knew that to lock eyes with one of these guys was seen as a serious challenge that could end up with one of them dead. With no hope of outrunning him, he avoided glancing in the guy's direction. They joined the march toward downtown with somebody coming up quick.

"Hey, asshole! Where ya going so fast?"

He could see the headline, *Failed Novelist Knifed for No Apparent Reason*. There would be an interview with Margo. "It was a useless death. He was dying from Parkinson's any way."

He chuckled to himself in spite of the situation. *Come at me, fuckhead. I have nothing to lose.*

Charlie could see the Marriott sign two blocks ahead; he listened for the guy's advancing footsteps. *What can I hit him with?* He could throw the laptop and make a run for it. *John would be pissed.*

He turned around to confront the man behind him and took a mental snapshot for the police report later. He was enormous, a wall of a man, in his thirties.

"Yeah? What do you want?"

"Got a light?" the stranger asked in a southern accent.

Charlie shook his head.

"Shit, I was warned y'all weren't a very friendly bunch, but you just proved it."

"Well, I don't know you. New York's full of hustlers and con artists."

"But I don't even sound like I'm from around here."

"New York's also home to a lot of unemployed actors and dialect coaches."

"Okay, I get ya. You got a ton of shit you're hauling there. Need a hand?"

Charlie studied his companion's round baby face. *In case I have to identify him later.*

"Nah, I'm good. Where ya headed?"

"I'm bunking at the Marriott." *Sure you are, buddy!*

"Do you always talk like a Roy Rogers knockoff?"

"Funny you should mention him. I'm Leroy Rogers, but my friends call me Skinny. Skinny Rogers, get it? I'm outta Lubbock, Texas."

Leroy looked like he weighed about 400 pounds. *What was I*

worried about? He'd be out of breath just trying to chase me.

"Why are you in New York, Leroy?"

"Skinny. Call me Skinny. I'm an undertaker. We gotta convention going on."

"That a fact? Skinny, can I ask you a question?"

"Shoot."

"I've been asking this all over the world: How do I get to the good place?"

"You'd have to ask my wife. She's the religious one. A real bible thumper. Don't get me wrong. I'm a God-fearing man, but I haven't done my homework for heaven like Lucy has."

"I don't suppose she came with you on this junket?"

"She joins me for one trip a year and this ain't it."

"Look, I'm going to hell in a handbasket and I need some answers." *Jesus, now he has me yapping like a good ol' boy.*

"Don't y'all have religious people here?"

"Oh yeah. We've got Pentecostals snake and no snake, Jews, Buddhists, Catholics, Scientologists, Seventh Day Adventists, Muslims, Hare Krishnas, Voodoo…"

"I get the picture. Might as well go looking on the Internet."

"I've done that too. Just give me some of that old-time religion. Any chance we can give your wife a jingle?"

"Well, my friend. I don't normally do this, but you seem a mite distraught and after four beers I'm saying no to nothing. What time would it be in Lubbock?"

"It's about 2 pm."

"Let's do this when we get to the hotel. I assume since you're hauling all that shit, you're staying at the Marriott, too?"

"I will be."

"I hope they have some rooms left. Our convention's pretty big."

"I'll buy you a beer when we get there."

"Good, 'cause I'm not feeling a buzz no more."

They had finally arrived. "Meet ya in the bar," said Skinny.

"I'm sorry, sir. There's a convention in town," the front desk clerk explained.

"So I heard. Can you hold my stuff for me while I figure out where I'm going?"

"Certainly, sir." The clerk called up house staff who took his belongings and handed him a claim check. Charlie headed to the bar.

He plopped down next to Skinny, his energy sapped from the walk and the bad news.

"You were right. I should have hung on to the room I had last night, but I really thought my wife was going to welcome me back with open arms."

"I know I just met you, hardly know you, but you seem all right. I've got two beds. I can pull 'em apart and let you have the other one."

"Wow, that's very generous of you, Skinny. Sure you can get by with just one?"

"Just be glad it's not a queen. By the way, I don't mean to pry, but what's your name?"

"Charlie. Charlie Wise," he said laughing.

Skinny's hand swallowed up Charlie's in a warm handshake. "Please to meet ya, Charlie. I done all the talking on the way here. It's your turn. How do you make a living?"

"Not very well. I'm a writer."

"What do you write?"

"I'm working on the Great American Novel. It's about me dying."

"I'd say this was destiny, Charlie. I can get you a helluva deal on a beautiful, mahogany casket, but I'm only authorized to bury you in the state of Texas." He looked Charlie up and down with sad brown eyes.

"And that's why you want to talk to my Lucinda."

"Yep."

"Let's get you a key to the room and head on up. I gotta check in with her anyhow. After that I've got a welcome party to go to. You can join me or get to writing."

"Actually, I'm re-reading the whole damn thing. There's something that's not working."

"In that case, you'd better grab a beer to go."

The room was cozy with the two of them in it.

"Let's get Lucy on the phone." He pulled out his cell and winked at Charlie as it rang.

"Hey, baby. Not much. Just sitting in the room before I go to some networking thing. Of course, I'll be drinking. I already started. I gotta guy here, a future customer, his name's Charlie, and he's looking for some answers. Mind talking to him?"

Skinny covered the phone. "She wants to know if you're a Christian. If you ain't, her answers may not apply."

"Jewish."

"Nope, Jewish," he told her. "Okay. Here's Lucy." He handed the phone to Charlie.

"Charlie, have you and my husband been drinking?"

"Yeah."

"You got a cell? I'm kinda busy at the moment. Give me your number. I'll call you back later."

Charlie rattled off his cell number and handed the phone back to Skinny. She had already hung up. Skinny checked the time and stood up.

"I'll leave you to it," Skinny said, "By the way, I snore."

"I'm not going to complain. You saved my ass."

"Nah. Lucy's going to do that. I'll get your ass later." Charlie looked at him blankly.

"Funeral humor."

Charlie grabbed the manuscript and sat on the edge of the bed with a pen to make notes. His phone rang.

"Hi, Charlie? It's Lucinda."

"Hi."

"What do you look like?"

"Huh?"

You Will Forever Be My Always

"It helps me visualize. How tall are you?"

"About five, ten."

"Weight?"

"What's that got to…"

"Weight?"

"About 220."

"Mmm," she purred. "What are you wearing?"

"What?!!"

"Scratch that. Just send me a naked selfie." His phone dinged. "That's one of me."

She was a little hefty, not anywhere near her husband's size, a platinum blonde with large breasts that sat atop a prodigious belly.

"What do you think?" she asked.

"Uh…" *Inappropriate?* "Very nice."

"Do you like dirty talk, Charlie?"

"Not really. I'm not very good at it."

"Where's that dick pic, Charlie? I'm a woman with needs!"

"Listen, Lucy. You seem very nice, but I'm not sure we should be doing this."

"Bullshit, Charlie. We're just having a conversation. You're not cheating on your wife. I'm not cheating on Leroy. Do you like blow jobs?"

"Uh, who doesn't?"

"Leroy does too. I just can't find the damn thing."

"I'm going to go now, Lucy. Have a good night."

He hung up before she could respond. *Weird.*

He gave himself a couple minutes to get composed. He deleted her picture from his phone. *No sense inviting trouble.*

He propped up the pillows and lay back as he sipped on his beer and started reading.

He woke up when he heard Skinny at the door. His watch said 10:30.

"How ya doing, Charlie?"

"Okay."

"Did you talk to Lucy? Was she able to help you out?" He made the universal masturbation gesture.

"What the hell, Skinny? Is that a thing you two do?"

Skinny chuckled. "Just harmless fun. It keeps us honest and faithful."

"You might have warned me."

"Your reaction's the best part. We get hours and hours of fun later with the recordings. Especially when she gets 'em going."

"Please erase mine."

"Will do. We always get rid of the duds. How's the reading going?"

"Slow. I'm not sure what I'm looking for."

"Do you mind if I read it? I read a lot."

"Do you have time? Aren't you supposed to be attending workshops or something?"

"Let me try. It's the least I can do for messing with your head."

"It can't hurt, I guess."

Charlie awoke the next morning and found a note next to the manuscript. "Pretty damn good so far. I got about 100 pages to go. See you at lunch time. Go ahead and order room service breakfast. It's on me."

He ate an omelet and dived back into the manuscript. He could tell something was "off," but he was too close to the forest to really see the trees, damn the cliches.

A knock on the door. "Are you decent?"

Skinny burst into the room. "Got a lunch to get to. I think I know what the problem is with your book. We'll talk later." And he was gone.

Frustrated, Charlie picked up the manuscript and continued where he had left off, more determined than ever to see whatever Skinny had seen.

Chapter 27

Charlie was watching the news when Skinny burst in about five. "Gonna have drinks in the bar. Care to join me?"

"Sure, but before we head downstairs tell me what you figured out!"

"Yeah. Okay. You wrote the book like it's finished. You can't write 'The End' without an ending."

"How am I supposed to write the ending when I'll be too dead to write it?"

"I'm no writer, but I think it's called a cliffhanger where you leave 'em guessing the ending."

Charlie stood there stunned. *How can I write an ending when there hasn't been one? God, I feel stupid.*

"You're absolutely right, my friend. Thank you. Drinks are on me."

It took him ten minutes the following morning – hangover and all – to fix the manuscript. He called Harvey to let him know he was on the way.

He didn't answer. Charlie tried again ten minutes later and ten after that, all the way over to his office.

As he hurried down the corridor, a stranger walked out of Harvey's office.

"Who are you?" he asked.

"I'm the building supe. Who are you?"

"Where's Harvey?"

"He had a heart attack last night. He died at the hospital this morning. Are you, were you a friend?"

Fucking fate! He didn't know if he should laugh at the cruel joke or cry at the loss of a dear friend.

"Yeah. A friend."

"You can call his daughter." He handed Charlie a business card with "Annabelle" and a number scribbled on the back. Harvey had a daughter? Who knew?

"Oh. Charlie. I'm so glad you called. I couldn't find your number in that fire hazard of an office. We're going to have services tomorrow. Can you make it?"

"Yeah. I'll be there."

He called Margo next. He broke down when she answered.

"Harvey's dead."

"Oh no! I'm so sorry, Charlie."

"They're having services tomorrow. Will you join me? Please?"

"Of course. Oh no! What about the book?"

"I can't think about that right now." But it was all he thought about in alternating moments of his grief.

"I'll see you tomorrow."

"Do you want company, Charlie? Do you want to come over?"

"I appreciate the offer, Margo, but I'm going to take care of some other stuff. We'll talk after services tomorrow."

"Okay."

He took a cab to John and Tina's. John had introduced him to Harvey twenty years ago when they were both still writing advertising copy and feeling like whores.

"I met this old yoshish at the schvitz the other day. He's got some stories."

"Please! John! Stop showing off your Yiddish!" Tina said.

"A funny old guy. Ira and I were schv… at the steam room and this guy was cracking us up. He's a literary agent from back in the day when they still used stone tablets."

They grew to be friends, but he never saw Harvey outside of his office. He wondered if he ever left. And now he had.

Tina leaned against her husband. He wrapped her in his arms

as though he could absorb her pain. "I loved that old schmuck," she sobbed.

"Please, Tina. I told you not to speak Yiddish. You're gonna say the wrong thing!"

"He was a cute little old man," she said.

"He always seemed like he was 90 years old."

"How old was he?"

"I don't know. I guess we'll find out."

"How can you know somebody for twenty years and know so little about him?"

All three of them shook their heads.

"Oh no! Charlie! What about your book?" Tina asked.

"We can't think about that now, Tina," John stated solemnly. "A man has died."

"The good news is I fixed what was wrong with it. The bad news is my agent died."

"Truly tragic."

"Yes."

Charlie stayed for dinner.

"How did Margo take it?" Tina asked.

"She was sad. She offered to have me come over to comfort me."

"Then why are you here?" John asked.

"I came to give you the bad news in person. It seemed the decent way of telling you."

"So, you told us. We grieved. Take this opportunity to go home again." John was practically shoving him out the door.

"I also had your laptop."

"It could have waited."

"Can't I spend the night here?"

"John, why don't you make us all a drink? We can toast to Harvey."

"You said you fixed the book?"

"Yes. It seemed so obvious when Skinny pointed it out to me."

"Who?"

"I'll explain later, but basically I wrote 'The End' and there wasn't one. Yet."

"You may have your ending now. You won the battle, but lost the war."

"John! You're being insensitive."

"No, he's got a point. I was waiting until after the funeral, after *shiva*, to suss this all out, but John's right. The book's chances at life died with Harvey."

"I don't believe that. It will find another agent and get published," said Tina.

"Margo has money. Self-publish," offered John.

"It's not really about the book. This whole exercise was to win back Margo's heart and the trust I destroyed. This manuscript was to put everything right so I could go to my grave with some chance of having cleared the slate."

Charlie's phone rang. "Margo?" asked Tina.

"It's a 512 number. Hello?"

"Charlie, it's Lucinda Rogers. I apologize for freaking you out last night."

"It's okay. It makes a weird sort of sense."

"Skinny's waiting for you back at the Marriott for a goodbye beer."

"Why didn't he call me?"

"He wanted to give me one more chance at that dick pic."

"I'm hanging up now."

"Just kidding, Charlie. He figured you were out roaming the countryside looking for a happy ending. Wow, I even made that sound dirty."

"Tell him I'm on my way. I'm going to impose on him one more time." He hung up before the conversation turned sexual again.

"You're free to stay the night here," offered John.

"No thanks. I'll see you at the funeral tomorrow."

Chapter 28

Charlie met Skinny in the bar.

"Just one bag tonight?"

"Yep. Going to a funeral tomorrow. Margo says I can come by in the morning and pick up a suit to wear."

"Who died?"

"My agent, damn him. I keep coming up with a great ending, but my life, and thus the book, keep on going."

"That's kind of a good thing, ain't it?"

"I guess."

"Remember, the point is to have your reader asking, 'What happens next?'"

"All the old cowboy movies had the hero riding off into the sunset. Nobody cared what happened next."

"So, what happens next?"

"I'm going to keep rewriting my ending till I get it right."

"What's that look like?"

"Getting Margo to take me back and maybe I'll continue my apology tour."

"Sounds like a 12-step kinda journey."

"Yeah, I guess." *Hi. I'm Charlie and I'm an asshole.*

"Who else is on the list? Is there a list?" Skinny, intrigued, ordered them another round and pulled out a notepad.

"There's a messed-up veteran in Houston named Arthur. And, oh Jesus. There's Patrice."

Charlie continued when Skinny raised an eyebrow.

"I can't believe I forgot about Patrice. The preacher's daughter.

We were both just 19. When she claimed she was pregnant, I called bullshit and left town."

"That's some major karma right there."

"If I'm going to apologize to every woman I screwed over, this is going to turn into a fulltime job."

"That's up to you, my friend."

"Oh my God! Ralph! When Randy had me ditch the weed the night we were raided, I gave it to Ralph to hold on to for the weekend. He got popped when he stopped for gas and a kilo fell out at the pump. A highway patrol cop was at the next pump."

"This trip could be fun, I mean interesting," Skinny remarked.

"I'm going to ask Margo to go with me. A road trip could be just the thing for talking this all out."

"I'm sure Margo would love to meet Patrice."

"Shit. That probably won't work."

"Not even in the best of times."

"I'd ask you to come along, but those bodies won't bury themselves."

"I don't do the actual burial and I have a business partner who can handle the funeral and administrative stuff. By the way, are your friend's services taken care of?"

"I really don't know. Do you also handle Jewish funerals?"

"We're talking Lubbock, man. We got Jews in Lubbock."

"I'm sure Annabelle doesn't want to bury him in Texas."

"Where's he from?"

"I don't know."

"Well, there ya go. Can't rule it out just yet."

Charlie called Annabelle. "Hi, it's Charlie. Do you need any help with the arrangements?"

"No. Thanks for the offer, though. My brother, my other brother's here to help."

Shit, Harvey had a son, too?

"We're starting at 10:30 am."

"Great. I mean okay, I'll be there. And Margo will be joining me. And John and Tina."

He jotted down the address and promised again they would all be there.

Charlie turned to Skinny. "Sounds like they've got it covered."

"Just trying to help. Hamakom y'nachem etchem b'toch sh'ar availai tziyon ee yerushalayim."

"What?"

"You're supposed to say that to the family. Here, I'll write it out phonetically for you."

"Wow. You're good."

"The best in Lubbock."

"One or two beers more. Then I should probably eat something."

"How about we call room service? I've got a joint up in the room."

"I thought possession meant hard time in Texas."

"You'd be surprised what ya find in the pockets of the dearly departed. Ya probably heard, 'Dead men tell no tales.' They don't smoke joints, either."

"I don't know if I should be doing this," Charlie confessed, holding in a hit and losing it in a paroxysm of coughing.

"If it kills ya, you've got your ending."

"But now I've got no book."

"One thing at a time, grasshopper. Let's get you through the next 24 first."

There was a knock at the door. "Room service."

"Oh, shit! What do I do with this?" Charlie asked, waving the remainder of the joint around.

"Allow me." Skinny opened the door to a smiling delivery man somewhere in his late twenties. He inhaled deeply as he rolled in the cart with two large steaks and baked potatoes. Skinny handed him the rest of the joint. "Keep the change!"

"Cool!"

They sat down to eat.

Charlie said, "I either get really philosophical or really paranoid about now."

"Let's get Lucy on the phone and talk about Heaven."

"This isn't going to be some kinky three-way, is it?"

Skinny guffawed. "That was probably funnier 'cause I'm high, but no. We're straight up this time."

"Before we get Lucy on the phone, Skinny, let's start with you. How long have you been an undertaker?"

"About ten years. I started as a gravedigger and worked my way up. Sorry, funeral humor."

"Moving on. Because of your job, have you ever felt closer to God?"

"Not really. It's like you dating that preacher's daughter. You're kinda one or two steps removed."

"Actually, God was probably pissed off about that one. I know her daddy was."

"What are you worried about? Y'all are the chosen people."

"Depends who you're talking to. So, no special insights? Nobody came back from the dead and said, 'Yep, Baptist is the way to go?'"

Skinny chuckled. "No, man. It's a humbling experience, thinking 'that's me in 20 years.' All that mystical shit goes out the window when you've got to exhume a body and you see a rotting corpse. There's bones and something gelatinous that used to be flesh. The Rapture when everybody's called up to Heaven is going to look pretty gruesome."

"I thought you said you were a God-fearing man. You sound more like an atheist."

"I fear Him every time I think I'm overstepping my bounds and questioning His wisdom or His existence. Lucy sets me straight. She's my pipeline."

"You know, I don't think we need to call Lucy. I think I've got all my answers."

"Oh shit. Now you've gone and screwed it up between God

and me. You see, Lucy works with me at the funeral parlor. She was planted there by the local Church of Jehovah. There are lots of folks who come there to bury a loved one and sometimes it's the first time they're looking eternity in the face. Lucy offers to pray with them, then they're talking Scripture, then she'll see them in church on Sunday. Works all the time. We're at 37 saved. Except for your tribe. Y'all are a loyal bunch."

"You two are an interesting couple."

"That we are, brother. Whataya say? One more beer, a little TV and some shuteye?"

Chapter 29

The next morning Charlie practically jumped out of bed in nervous anticipation of the day's events. First, there were the many moods of Margo. Just after lights-out Annabella had texted a request for a few words from him at the services. "K," he responded, an exchange that put off sleep while he jotted down a few ideas. He nodded off for just a second and checked the last sentence he had scribbled: Perspiration skills. *That's the end of that.* He shut off his bedside lamp and hoped he would dream of the perfect eulogy.

Was his eulogy waiting for him the next morning, perfectly prepared for him by his subconscious? Hell no. He looked at Skinny snoring, oblivious to his predicament. He checked his phone for messages. There was one – a text at 1:05 am from – Leroy Rogers?

Need a eulogy? a few funerals ago. Everybody crying happy tears.

There was a file attached that he opened immediately and quickly scanned. *Hey, this is pretty good!*

Charlie took a shower and put on Margo's favorite cologne before taking a taxi to the house. He noticed their postage stamp-sized lawn was sprouting ankle-height weeds. At the door, he listened to the clear dulcet tones of the doorbell echo around the foyer.

A man he'd never met answered the door completely naked. "You must be Charlie…" *And you must be dizzy with all the blood rushing to that monstrosity.*

Margo appeared next to him wearing a bathrobe. "I apologize, Charlie. Let me grab your suit. The black one?" Her voice came from the bedroom – *their* bedroom.

She came to the door and saw open hostility on the two men's faces.

"Playing nice, boys? Charlie, I also packed a bag with some socks, underwear, and your nice black shoes. Can you think of anything else?"

How I'd like to wipe the smirk off your boyfriend's face. "No thanks. You've done enough. Guess I'll see you there."

"I could drop you both off at the mortuary on my way to the gym. You could Uber it home afterward."

"I've got a cab waiting. I'll see you there." Charlie locked eyes with Margo. "Please don't be late."

The Uber driver was a blonde millennial girl with a nose ring.

"Sorry. I don't usually do this, but I have to change in your back seat. I'm on my way to a funeral."

"Don't flatter yourself, dude. You're old enough to be my grandfather."

His dignity was taking assaults on all fronts. "No, don't flatter YOURSELF, DUDE. I wouldn't touch you even with the schmekel I just saw. And believe me you would be impressed!"

Charlie pulled on his suit coat. He unbuckled his pants and reached for his suit pants. The girl, Mandy, it said on his app, pulled over and slammed on the brakes.

"Sir, I have to ask you to put your clothes back on!"

"What? I told you I'm on my way to a funeral and I'm changing back here."

"Sir, shall I just drive my vehicle to the 49th precinct? You're this close to sexual assault."

"I don't have time for this shit! You know what? Yeah! Let's go. I can probably change there."

She fiddled with her GPS slowly while studying him in her review mirror.

"Old guys like you make me sick."

"Yeah, we're all wrinkly and our balls get wet every time we take a dump."

"Keep talking, asshole. You're going to jail."

They pulled into the police station's parking lot. "Get out!" she hissed.

"What?"

"We're here."

He opened the car door and had barely enough time to scoop up his belongings before she slammed the door with the force of her exit.

Charlie walked up to the desk sergeant. "Some crazy woman just dropped me off here. I need a bathroom to change and a way to get to Brighton for a funeral."

"Restroom's around the corner. Subway's down the street."

"Good enough. I'll change and be on my way."

Charlie admired himself in the bathroom mirror. He thought he looked his best in a suit and just because it was for a somber occasion it didn't mean he didn't look positively James Bondian.

He flashed back to his confrontation with Margo and her well-endowed lover. *She had better show without him!* His ego couldn't handle another beat-down. At least now he understood her reluctance to get back together. *Good for you, Margo. You stopped waiting around for my return.*

The room had ten people in it with the inclusion of Charlie. *When all your friends go before you, there's hardly anybody left to note your passing. And if you've pissed everyone off along the way, there will be even fewer.*

He was happy/relieved to see that Margo had come alone. He spotted John and Tina at the same time they noticed his entrance. John pointed across the aisle to a vacant seat next to Margo.

She looked up when he stood over her. "Is this seat taken?"

"Dick's in the restroom." She saw his crestfallen look. *Self-esteem: direct hit!* "Just kidding. Please join me."

"So, his name is Dick? Really?"

They both chuckled. "No," she replied. "It's Richard." They couldn't contain the laughter without bursting. They made a dash for the door. They both laughed until it hurt. Finally, Charlie got his breath back.

"At least it isn't Willie!" The comment once again incapacitated them as they laughed and snorted and laughed some more.

"God, I needed that," Margo said.

"Can we get coffee after this?"

"I have to get home. We're headed to MOMA."

"Just a quick cup?"

The conversation was interrupted by the arrival of Annabelle and her brother.

"Charlie, this is my brother, Aaron. He's a rabbi and he'll be leading the services today."

"Of course. Welcome, rabbi."

"Just call me Aaron. We're practically family."

"This is my … This is Margo."

He shook her hand by the fingers. "I so glad you could be here today."

"Thanks," she said. "It's nice to be reminded why I married him."

"That and my overwhelming schmekel."

"And that will be the reason I divorce him." She turned to Charlie. "Some things should be kept in the bedroom."

"Tell that to your houseguest!"

The rabbi was trying desperately to interject and move along, but Charlie had one last thing to say, "Hamakom y'nachem etchem b'toch sh'ar availai tziyon ee yerushalayim."

"Thank you very much." The rabbi had finally found closure to their argument and slipped away to greet others.

"Sorry."

"It started out as a compliment then you made it something dirty."

"Sorry, sorry, sorry." *I don't think I have any more apologies in me. Throw that Jewish guilt right back on her. Don't let up! The enemy's engaged!*

"I was going to invite you on a road trip. Before I die."

She rolled her eyes. "What makes you think I would have gone?" *Ouch!* "As you have seen, I have a lot on my hands." *That was below the belt.*

Last resort. Lower the drawbridge. "I wanted to have a chance to really, really communicate. Just you, me, and the open road."

"And?" she asked.

"And?"

"I trust we wouldn't be driving around aimlessly."

"No. I've got a lot of people in my past, some cliffhangers that need an ending. It's my apology tour."

Annabelle walked up at that moment. "We're ready to begin."

"I'll be right back," he promised.

Charlie strode to the front of the room. He looked around frantically for Harvey's casket. *Oh yeah, Jewish services. No casket. Too many funerals in the last few months.*

"Harvey Goldman was my friend, my uncle, my mensch. When I left advertising to write the great American novel, Harvey tried to tell me I had a hard road ahead. He even tried to get my Margo to talk me out of it and go back to a fat paycheck that would support the lifestyle we had grown to love and appreciate. Margo knew how much this dream meant to me. She wouldn't let me quit, even after the months turned to years.

"Harvey and I were brothers from different mothers. We both had gambling sprees in our pasts, got knocked down hard by reality and a couple big gangster types, and ended up across the desk from each other swapping stories.

"I have to share some of the last, best advice Harvey had for me: 'Stay away from the tear-jerkers.' I think he would say the same today. L'Chayim."

Rabbi Aaron whispered, "That comes later. When we drink to his life."

Aaron's admonishment threw Charlie for a moment as he searched his script to find where he had left off. "This sweet man had a daughter, Annabelle and a son, Aaron. Aaron is a rabbi and will tell us more of his father's life."

Charlie walked back to sit beside his wife and found the seat empty. He walked out as she drove away.

He dialed her cell number. "Yes?"

"Why did you run out like that? What's going on?"

"I have some loose ends to tie up before I can leave town."

"Oh."

He danced a little jig of happiness and suddenly remembered where he was. He went back to the services with a small smile threatening to spill across his face.

Chapter 30

After the services Charlie begged off dinner and the start of sitting shiva, mirrors covered all around the house, for the next seven days. He went back to the hotel to share the good news with Skinny.

"Damn. I have to tell ya I'm kinda disappointed I'm not going to be riding shotgun, but I'm happy for you and your lady. Remember, if things get tense and you're passing through Lubbock about that time, she can stay with Lucy while you and me *Easy Rider* our way through Texas."

He texted Margo. **Ready for some company?**

Not yet. Problem still here.

Need help?

No. Just a little time and space. God, men are so clingy!

Charlie turned to Skinny. "Can you put up with me one more night?"

"You're buying dinner!"

Over seafood they talked about Charlie's plans.

"I envy you, Skinny. Your life is so much simpler than mine. In Lubbock you've got, what, one-tenth the population of greater Manhattan. You work in a mortuary, a nice quiet environment…"

"Don't you realize that we undertakers come here from far and wide to add a little excitement to our lives? This little donnybrook has provided me some insight into the locals. Like you. I got to know a New Yorker inside out and up close!"

"The pace will kill you."

"It's not normal to have all these people living atop one another.

No wonder y'all have so many neuroses and so many psychiatrists to treat 'em. To us out-of-towners, this is like going to an amusement park. It's fun, but you wouldn't want to live there."

"I'm glad you understand that. I'm glad I met you, Skinny. You also gave me a glimpse into the heart of the heartland."

"Thanks, but you're still picking up the check."

Chapter 31

"Thanks, doc, for squeezing me in on short notice."

"So, what's going on, Charlie?"

"I'm feeling really sad and can't seem to shake it off."

"What's happening in your life? Any triggers for depression?"

He explained his quest for information and his other quest for forgiveness. He told her about his suicide attempt in Thailand, his epiphany in Morocco. He talked about the death of his friend and the realization that after 20 years, he hadn't really known him. He described how Margo had finally cheated and was now willing to kick out a better man to travel across country with him.

"Lots of triggers there. Would you be willing to try an antidepressant?"

"It doesn't thrill me. All I need is another pill."

"This drug should help you."

"What about side effects?"

"We have to fine-tune the dosage right away or your depression could get worse and make suicide a possibility."

"Great. What else?"

"You could have hallucinations and delusions."

"Parkinson's. Next."

"Dizziness, lack of consciousness…"

"Parkinson's. How will I know if my symptom is the disease or the so-called cure?"

"There are other possibilities."

"You mean other drugs. No thanks. Right now I know for sure my depression is from the disease. I'd rather smoke a joint, pour a glass of wine, and chill in front of the TV. Thanks anyway, Doc."

"It sounds like you may have a substance abuse issue."

"You can't OD on pot. Wine doesn't make you suicidal. I'll take my chances."

Leaving the neurologist's office, he called Margo. "Got your suitcase packed?"

"I've got *his* suitcase packed. I called him a taxi."

"I'm picking up a rental car. I'll see you in an hour, okay?"

There was a sigh on the other end. "Do you still want to do this?" he asked.

"It's not so much I *want* to. I *need* to."

"Why is that?"

"I need to give us another chance."

He bit his lip to hold back the tears. "I love you, Margo."

"Fuck me. I love you, too, Charlie."

He showed an hour later in a roomy Cadillac SUV. With a spring in his step, he rang the doorbell. She opened the door and hugged him tightly, a warm embrace that lasted several seconds. *This is a good omen.*

"Is he gone?" he asked.

"Long gone."

"Ready to go?"

"Sure."

It was a bright Spring day in April. He carried her luggage to the car and turned to look at her. He could see the college professor who had enchanted him 30 years before. *Who knows? Mr. Happy could make a surprise appearance tonight!*

"You look handsome," she said, brushing back his hair.

The casual touch of her hand was anything but casual. It sent a pulse of electricity up his arm. He hadn't realized until just this moment how much he had missed that touch.

"Margo, I'm struck speechless right now."

"Not good news for a writer."

"Or a romantic moment."

"Let's take it slow and easy. We've got miles to go. We could be at each other's throat by the time we reach Philly."

"I wish now I had rented a convertible. You would look so Grace Kelly with your beautiful hair streaming behind you in the wind."

"And have it look like a tumbleweed in five minutes? No thanks! This is perfect. This car is gorgeous and more comfortable than our living room."

"It's got a great sound system. Listen to this!" He had prepared a playlist of all their favorites.

Five miles later, Margo leaned over and lowered the volume. "I thought we were going to talk."

I'm not ready for this.

"Shoot."

"Where in Texas are we going?"

"I grew up in a little town outside Houston. I've got three people to see."

"Tell me a story, Charlie. Tell me about a poor little boy in the south."

"I escaped."

"I don't think that poor little boy ever did, Charlie."

"You mean because I can't let this shit go and be done with it?"

"Because you haven't realized that any kindness is quickly forgotten and that damage can never be undone."

"I've been all over the world asking questions about salvation and all along I had my very own Bubbe buddha."

"Charlie, this is one of those times when your joke sounds like you're making fun of me."

"What? Oh no, honey. I just wanted a reason to say bubbe buddha. It sounds like something's boiling on the stove."

"You know what, Charlie. I'm just too old and tired to fly off into a rage like I used to. That's why I thought a revenge fuck might make me feel better, like I beat you at your own game."

Always competitive. Always has to be right. Maybe if I stick to screaming under my breath, we can still have a great time.

"Can I make one more dick joke?" He pointed to the NOW LEAVING THE STATE OF NEW YORK sign. "Schlong, New York." She hid a smile and shook her head.

The GPS directed him to the 81 highway that would take them toward Philadelphia, but some memories were stirring and he stayed on I-95 south.

When they hit the outskirts of Baltimore, Charlie gently nudged Margo awake.

"How about lunch?"

She looked around and figured out where they were immediately. "Sounds divine!"

He took her to a place they had visited on the way to Florida one summer. He remembered the red umbrellas out front and their famous crab cakes.

Margo full of fun and energy. *Maybe I'm feeling some of that, too.*

Neither one of them could remember a seafood meal quite so delicious. An hour later they were back on I-95 and starting to run into traffic around Washington, D.C.

Margo noticed Charlie periodically checking his watch. "Do you have an appointment somewhere?"

"Shh. It's a secret!"

Traffic began to lighten up just south of the capitol as they moved into Virginia. The train station was on the other side of the expressway.

"What are we doing here?" she asked.

"Remember how we always talked about that romantic train ride we were going to take some day? That's today!"

She clapped her hands like an excited child and grinned. "What about this big, beautiful car?"

"It's coming with us," he answered. "We're non-stop on the train to Orlando. We'll have to backtrack a bit once we get there to start heading west, but I'm okay with that. How about you?"

"Please tell me you got us a sleeper car."

"I did."

"Then yes!" They pulled into the lot and dropped off the car with an attendant.

She looked at him with gratitude that bordered on tears. He couldn't tell if he had reached her heart yet. "Thanks, Charlie."

"You're welcome." *If I had known how much this trip would mean to you, we would have done it a long time ago.* He smiled down at her.

"You've changed, Charlie. I like it."

They boarded the train with their essentials and found their sleeper car. The attendant showed them how the bed pulled out and all the amenities. He explained meals, the observation car and the bar car. Then he left them alone.

"Want to go grab a drink?" he asked, secretly anxious to explore.

She had been with him long enough to know he wanted to prowl. "Why don't you go get both of us something?"

He returned with red wine for her and beer for him. They sat across from one another as the train slowly rolled out of town. All they could see for the time being was a series of industrial buildings covered in graffiti. "This is nice." She couldn't believe his transformation. She was afraid something would come up to spoil the mood.

"So, after Orlando, what then?"

"We head north on the I-75 north to the 10 west…"

"And what about when we reach Texas? Where are we going then?"

"Well, first there's Ralph."

By the time the attendant tapped on the door to announce dinner, she was fully versed on Ralph's three-year stint in Fishkill Prison.

"That doesn't really sound like your fault, Charlie. He was just stupid."

"Yeah, but he wouldn't have been carrying those 20 keys if I hadn't asked him to hold on to them for a couple of days."

"If this is for the book…"

"Not anymore."

They stopped talking as they traversed the narrow hallway of the swaying sleeper car. More couples and families were leaving their rooms for dinner and crowding the walk space.

They were greeted and seated within minutes. Charlie lifted a fresh beer. "Here's to an interesting trip with the love of my life."

"An interesting, *awarding* trip with closure for you."

"Amen. Thanks."

As they finished dinner, Charlie suggested the observation car and a nightcap. *I really shouldn't be drinking so much, but I'm not driving.* He also was nervous. Every minute with Margo an inevitable argument endangered the precarious rapport of the moment.

They sat and stared out at a pitch-black nighttime landscape.

"So, what did you learn on your travels, Charlie?"

"So much, Margo. You read a lot of it in the book."

"Don't get mad if I ask some questions, okay?"

Uh oh. Here it comes. "Sure. Ask away."

"You won't get mad?"

"This is me being an open book. No pun intended."

Occasionally, they were distracted by the lights of a town.

"Did you love the woman in Thailand?"

"No."

"But you used the word in the book."

"I've thought about that. I loved the way she treated me. At first, vain male that I am, I thought there was an attraction there. Boy, was I wrong!"

"What about all those other women, the ones *not* in the book?"

"I tried to explain that in the book. All meaningless ways to drive us further apart. You had, I mean, the relationship had gone cold…"

"So, you still blame me?"

"You asked me if these questions were going to make me mad.

Are they pissing you off?"

"They're stirring up some old feelings."

"I used to blame you. Not anymore. We both freaked out after the miscarriage and tried to pretend nothing happened."

There were tears in her eyes. "Do you have to keep bringing that up?"

I think you're in denial with a touch of PTSD. "No. Let's let it go."

"I think I'm ready for bed."

"Me too."

They made their way back to their room. "Shower?" he asked her.

"You go ahead."

The attendant had turned their sofa into a bed; he found he still had room to take off all his clothes. The water was warm at best, but it left him feeling refreshed and drowsy. When he came out Margo was lying with her body turned toward the wall.

"Your turn." No response. She was either asleep or pretending. Either way, there would be no further discussion.

"Can we spoon?" she asked in the darkness. He slid over and draped an arm over her. "I don't want you falling off this little bed."

Chapter 32

Charlie woke to golden, dappled sunlight streaming into the room. He was alone in the bed, alone in the room.

The door slid open; Margo had a cup of coffee in each hand. "Good morning. They're serving breakfast right now. We're getting to Sanford train station at about nine."

He sat up and stretched, still fascinated by the golden glow that lit the room. It gave her a radiance, a corona that reminded him of Renaissance paintings of the virgin Mary.

"I'm starving." As he swung his legs over to stand up, a cramp seized the tendons of his right leg, a squeeze that forced him to groan at the sharp intensity of it. Margo massaged his leg until the pain was bearable and he was able to stand.

Over breakfast, she asked, "I take it that cramp was part of the Parkinson's experience?"

Charlie nodded.

"Is this the first time this has happened to you?"

"No."

"Do you want to go home?"

"No. In fact, it motivates me."

"Then let's press on."

"When we get to Sanford, we'll get the car and head north on I-75 till we get to the 10 West through Alabama, Mississippi, then Louisiana and on into Texas. If we wanted to, we could take that highway all the way to the Pacific Ocean."

They repacked their overnight bags. "Just in time," Charlie commented as the train began to slow.

They claimed the car. Finding the road north was easy with the GPS.

"Tallahassee." Charlie turned to Margo. "We have to get gas for this behemoth. Ready for lunch?"

"Sure," she said.

"Pull up something on your phone."

"I think you'll like this place. Just follow my directions."

When they pulled up, Charlie laughed. "The Midtown Caboose?"

Over a hearty lunch, Margo noticed Charlie hand was shaking. "Did you take your meds today?"

"I forgot them."

"Jesus, Charlie! On the train, at the hotel?"

"I was so busy making reservations for the car and the train, they just slipped my mind."

"We're going to this place, Patients First. No appointment needed."

The office was on a major thoroughfare and the staff seemed friendly.

"I'm not a neurologist, Mr. Wise," Dr. Peters demured.

"I'm not asking for one. Just call mine. Her name's Brain."

Charlie was disappointed when the name failed to elicit a chuckle.

"Not funny?"

"Not around here when we've got Dr. Beaver the gynecologist."

Dr. Peters spoke to Charlie's neurologist and scribbled out his prescriptions.

"Your neurologist tells me memory issues are par for the course. She suggested you set alarms on your phone to remind you when you're supposed to take 'em. Pharmacy's pretty close. Good luck to you, sir, ma'am."

A half hour later they were back on the road west. "You need to take care of yourself, babe."

Oh my God, a term of endearment!

"I know. Sorry. I was just so excited about this trip with you." He glanced at the sign they were about to pass. "We just passed Pensacola. It's four o'clock. Kinda early to stop for dinner, right?"

"What's the next big city?"

"Mobile, Alabama. About an hour ahead. It will put us on the 10."

They picked a place near the highway, the Fort Conde Inn. "It looks like a plantation," Margo remarked. She marveled at the fireplace in their room. She perused the breakfast menu. "Breakfast is included. For a little extra, we can get breakfast in bed!"

Charlie looked at the menu over her shoulder. "Classy place. You have to speak French to order anything."

"Let's go check out the harbor area."

His legs had been bothering him all day, but he wasn't going to rain on her parade.

"Lead the way."

They decided a place on the marina looked inviting and it was very close. They ordered drinks and were surprised when the family at the table next to them bowed their heads and an old man began, "Oh heavenly Jesus…"

Margo rolled her eyes until Charlie scowled at her. A scruffy looking redheaded teenager sat among the prayerful family and stared straight ahead at them. "That kid's giving me the creeps," she whispered.

"Just ignore him."

The family kept the waitress busy running to the kitchen when something was not to their liking, extra mustard, more napkins. The teen seemed very interested in Margo and Charlie. They talked about the next leg of the trip.

"I was going to wait and surprise you, but we have an opportunity to make a detour to New Orleans. I know you've always wanted to go. It might be disappointing; we missed Mardi Gras."

"Oh, but the history!"

"I'll take that as a yes."

The family at the next table looked to be finishing up at the same time they were. "You'd better hurry," Margo whispered. "You don't want to be behind them while they're arguing about the check." Charlie practically ran to the cashier.

"Your prices made me homesick for New York."

"Surprise!" the cashier said. "We've got a whole lot cheaper menu for the locals."

"Funny!"

They were in the parking lot when the teen ran up to them. "Y'all looking to get high?"

"No!" said Margo.

"What do you have in mind?" Charlie asked.

"Got three joints of some chronic."

"How much?"

"Charlie!"

He was inspecting one of the kid's joints. "Great, now he knows my name. We're going to have to kill him."

The teen blanched. "Relax," said Charlie. "I was just kidding. How much?"

"One for five, two for $12, three for $15."

"Explain that to me."

"If you smoke the first one, you're going to want the other two. I already know that, so I'm charging extra for the second one and meet you halfway on the third. The price could go up in a minute if you dillydally."

"I'll give you $15 for the three. And another $5 for that imagination."

"Deal!"

After he was gone, Charlie turned to Margo. "The entrepreneurial spirit is alive in that boy."

"So is price gouging."

He shrugged.

"Why did you buy pot?"

"Remember that horrible leg cramp I had this morning? They're getting to be pretty regular. I don't want to get addicted to opioids so this is the best thing I've found to deal with the pain."

"So, it takes away your pain?"

"No. I'm just so stoned I *forget* I'm in pain."

She just shook her head.

"I'm saving it for tonight and a little in the morning. One joint will last me three days. Believe me. The stuff they smoke these days can leave you catatonic!"

They walked hand-in-hand around the harbor and back to the inn.

"I really want breakfast in bed tomorrow morning."

"Your wish is my command."

"It's a little muggy. Feel like a nap?" She winked.

"I'm not really…oh." He wasn't sure he was up to the task. *I don't want to fail and have her look at me that way.*

"No pressure. We'll take things slow and easy. Did you take all your meds?"

"Yes. Thanks for asking. Even the little blue one." He grinned.

"That little blue one you took in chapter three of your book?"

She really read it!

"Actually, this is an organic compound I picked up in Thailand." He registered the disappointed look on her face. "But never used. I was waiting for now. It's not going to shoot my blood pressure through the ceiling, I promise."

"Wait. Is this premeditated spontaneous sex? Am I just part of your diabolical scheme?"

"Totally." He felt a stirring in his pants. "What sounds better: 'The beast awakens!' or 'Houston, we have liftoff?'"

"Neither. I say, 'Run for the fun!'"

They both tried for a dignified scramble to the room. Once inside, they tore at each other's clothes until they were naked and out of breath.

She held his organ in her hand. It was the hardest she had seen in several years. "Slow," she whispered.

He didn't respond; he just held her soulful eyes in his gaze. Suddenly everything went black.

He came to on the floor surrounded by hotel staff, Margo, and several EMTs. He looked down. *Yep, still naked. Still hard, too.*

"What happened?" he asked.

"Your blood pressure dropped significantly, sir. Have you taken any uh, supplements this afternoon?"

He just nodded.

"It probably reacted with one of your other, uh, medicines. Just take it easy. Your afternoon isn't totally ruined. You've still got that impressive erection. Give us a call if it won't go away."

The little cluster of concerned folks murmured, "Glad you're okay. Be careful. Take care," and seemed to vanish as one.

"I'm so fucking embarrassed."

"It doesn't seemed to have affected you too badly."

How am I going to walk out of here tomorrow?

"Are you still in the mood?" she asked sweetly.

"I was just lying there naked with that thing pointing due north."

Margo start giggling. "Sorry. Couldn't stop myself."

"You've embarrassed him," Charlie said, acting offended.

"I guess I'll just have to look him in the eye and apologize."

"Do you think you two could kiss and make up?"

"I think that could be arranged."

They woke two hours later and Charlie was relieved the swelling had subsided.

"It's dark outside. What time is it?"

"Seven."

"We should go find a restaurant. I don't think they stay up late around here."

"Charlie, can we just order a pizza and watch some TV?"

"Okay."

The pizza was shards of crust and they had sat through another romcom before Margo decided it was time to talk.

"Let's take a joint out on the balcony," she suggested.

"I could use a couple hits."

"Pain?" she asked.

"A little. Just want to feel a little numb."

Two puffs each and they put the rest away for another time.

"Are you okay?" she asked.

"What a day, huh?"

"Something we'll laugh about later."

"I really liked what happened after that."

"Me too. We're still not quite caught up," she said.

"I know. You've got questions. Stuff in the book or who we're going to see?"

"Pick one and go with it."

"How about Arthur?"

"Who is, who was Arthur? Wait a minute. Was he James in the book?"

"Yeah."

"An arm and a leg, really?"

"Yeah."

"Okay. And…?"

"That's enough for tonight. I'm bushed. Can we just relax and watch some brain-numbing TV?

"Okay."

"I love you, Margo."

"Love you, too. I just want you to know this is a brave thing you're doing here."

"Thanks."

Chapter 33

"Patrice." They had had breakfast in bed, checked out and were on the road for a half hour when he sprang the next name on her.

"Who?"

"Patrice Harrison."

"That name sounds familiar. I think you mentioned her once a long time ago. Some old college girlfriend."

"Yeah, well, there's a little more to the story."

"Do tell."

"We were stupid kids. She told me she was pregnant. I didn't believe her. I came back to New York."

"Was she?"

"Nah. Probably not."

"*Probably* not? Jesus, Wise, you've been an asshole for a very long time. Are we going to meet a son who looks a lot like you?"

"Let's just say on the off chance she wasn't lying to keep me from leaving, he – or she – would be 41. If such a person exists, they've flown the nest a long time ago."

"Okay, okay. Let's not talk for a while, all right?"

He shrugged, not looking at her, eyes on the road.

"Look, she had my parents' number and address in New York…"

"Please. Shut up."

He turned on the radio. She shut it off.

Fuck New Orleans. But he still took the turnoff.

Margo spotted the Welcome sign. "If you're trying to smooth

everything over, it's not going to work."

"Not my intent."

They parked at a public lot near Bourbon Street and went searching for a coffee shop nearby.

"It smells like piss around here."

I don't smell anything. "Funny. They didn't mention it in the brochure."

She spun around to face him. "Look, I'm going shopping. Why don't you do your own thing for about an hour and meet me back here?"

"You don't want me to go with you?"

"I need some space. Just give me an hour, okay?"

"Fine." When she went straight, he turned right and veered back toward the car.

He climbed behind the wheel and pulled the used joint from its hiding place. The car didn't have a lighter. They had passed a 7-11 coming into town about two blocks back. His legs were already beginning to ache.

He walked out of the store with two lighters, a powerball ticket and a pink sno-ball. He was ready for an attack of the munchies. As soon as he was far enough away from anybody, walking back to the car, he pulled out the joint and lit up. A cop on a motorcycle come up from behind him and zipped by. *Keep going, keep going.*

The cop u-turned and came up to Charlie.

"Smells like skunk."

"Yeah, I think somebody must have hit one back there."

"Haha. Hand me the drugs, sir."

The cop removed his helmet. Charlie handed over the still-burning joint.

"License and registration."

"I'm not in a car."

"License for now then. I'll get your registration at your vehicle."

Charlie handed over his license. "Why do you need to see my

registration? I'm not driving."

"Not at the moment. But judging from what I saw, you will be high when you get behind that wheel within the next two hours, so I'm being proactive. I'm issuing you a ticket for possession."

"A ticket?"

"Within the city limits of New Orleans, possession of marijuana is a misdemeanor. It's like a traffic ticket. You can pay the fine right now for $100 or you can wait till court opens and file for a trial and maybe get it dropped to a $40 fine. It's your call."

"Let's take care of this now." The cop carried on as Charlie dug out the cash.

"Sir, you are very fortunate to have broken the law in New Orleans. In Louisiana proper, you might have been facing jail time. Which vehicle is yours?"

"The Escalade."

"Nice car."

"Thanks."

"Are you packing any more contraband?"

"Nope. That was it." *Don't search the car.*

The cop leaned in and took a whiff. "Nope. It still has that new car smell. I'm coming by in an hour, then again in another hour. I expect to see you sitting there."

"What about lunch or the bathroom?"

"You may spend the next hour any way you wish, but I'll see you in 60 minutes. I don't want you driving around my city while under the influence. Have a good stay in New Orleans, sir." He drove off.

Twenty minutes later, Charlie headed to their rendezvous point. *Don't be late. Don't be late.*

She was waiting for him. "You reek. Smoking already?"

"Yeah. Pain."

"It's still too early for lunch. Let's just get back on the road."

"Would you mind driving for a while? My legs are killing me."

"Do you know how long it's been since I drove a car?"

Please don't remind me! "It's like riding a bicycle. Besides, this car practically drives itself."

She adjusted the seat, the steering wheel, the mirrors, the moon roof, and her individual temperature control before she hesitantly shifted into drive.

The motorcycle cop came around the curve as Margo was looking for an opportunity to exit the lot. He quickly assessed the new driver and Charlie in the passenger seat and gave the thumbs up.

"The police around here seem very nice," Margo commented.

Chapter 34

Back on the road, Charlie made some calculations on his phone. "We should reach Houston in about six hours."

"That's what the car says, too," replied Margo, pointing to the GPS ETA on the dash.

"Oh, right."

"We haven't discussed Morocco."

A weary sigh escaped his lips. "Go ahead."

"What happened?"

"What do you mean, what happened? It's all in the book."

"What's *not* in the book, Charlie?"

"Oh Jesus. *I'm* the one with Parkinson's. *I'm* the one who's susceptible to delusions! After that indulgence in vanity in Bangkok, you know, where I tried to *kill* myself, plus my *plumbing* problems, I have a different perspective on sex. It doesn't rule my life anymore. And I really don't miss it that much."

Margo was quiet for a very long time.

"I don't think I've ever told you this whole story: Do you know how a Jewish family like my mom, John, and I ended up in Texas?"

"You said your mom had a bad marriage."

"Bad? It was the worst! It was the shits! Hank couldn't decide if he loved us or hated us. Nana and Papa were so pissed my mom married a goy, an uncultured, anti-intellectual goy, they wrote her off. He dragged us all the way across the country, then finally decided he hated us.

"Mom had to call and beg her folks to let us back in the family. We showed 'em our bruises and broken arms and they said God was teaching us a lesson to stay with our own kind."

"Wow."

"Everybody has a bad childhood," said Charlie.

"No, not everybody."

"Your parents were cool. I liked them."

They sat with their individual thoughts for a few more miles. "If I see one more Cracker Barrel sign, I'm going to stop."

"Where are we?" Charlie asked.

"Some place called Lafayette."

They drove around looking for a lunch spot with curb appeal. "Have you ever noticed how one place looks like another these days?"

"So, you want to eat at a franchise?"

"No, but I do have to pee. Like right now!"

"Denny's it is."

She found them a seat while Charlie ran to the restroom, almost tripping over a kid in a wheelchair. He returned looking distressed.

"Something wrong?"

"I almost made it." He showed her spots on the front of his pants.

"I'll order for you. Go get a change of clothes out of the car."

"Okay. Thanks."

He showed up redressed as the waitress brought their meals.

"Sorry."

"Shit happens." She paused. "It wasn't, was it?"

"No!"

"I ordered you chicken fried steak. Hope that's okay."

"It seems kinda silly to be watching my weight or cholesterol these days."

"You know you're probably going to outlive me, right?"

"It doesn't feel like it."

"What do you say we eat and run? I'd like to hit Houston before dark."

"I can take over driving," he offered.

"I kinda like the feel of all that power under me. You don't mind, do you?"

"Mind if I burn a little before we take off? You can join me."

"None for me, thanks. I'm driving."

He lit the second joint and inhaled deeply.

"How bad is your pain today?"

"What pain?" He grinned and coughed, exhaling a large cloud of smoke.

"Are you done?"

"Yeah, let's go. We should be there in about four hours."

"I know. The next couple days might be a little rough on you. Why don't you try to get some rest?"

"And if I'm sleeping, I can't criticize your driving. And you can't hammer me with questions."

"There's that, too."

"Wake me up for any reason."

"Sure."

She sat alone with her thoughts. The next few days would make them or break them. Despite all the tense moments when they traveled around the world and something went wrong, she secretly relied on his confident strength to get them through.

Already several times during this trip she had found renewed hope in their future together only to be shaken by some personality flaw that bobbed to the surface. She still loved him; that was her personality flaw.

She opened the window to get some fresh air and was rewarded with a blast of hot and humid. Dusk was coming and the headlights decided to turn on.

They were entering the outskirts of Houston when Charlie sat up. "Where are we?"

"So, now I get snoring and drool, too? We're in Houston."

"Cool." He wiped his sleeve across his mouth.

"Where are we staying?"

"Not sure yet." He pulled up an app on his phone and found something centrally located in their price range. "God bless the internet." It was another Marriott so he was getting points.

They checked in and unpacked. Margo lay back on the queen bed. "I'm so exhausted, maybe too exhausted for dinner, even."

"Gotta eat."

"Okay, but take your meds right now before you forget."

"Yes, dear."

They found a place recommended by the hotel's front desk clerk both intimate and quiet. They ordered dinner and Charlie reached to hold Margo's hand, but she pulled back.

"I'm not the same guy who took off on Patrice."

"I realize that, but your record toward women has been far from exemplary ever since."

"I deserved that. Do you think there's any chance of me going to Heaven?"

"I'll give you an answer when I see how you deal with these people from your past. Have you decided who you're going to see first and what you're going to say?"

"I'm going to start with Ralph. I think he's got a forgiving spirit."

"What the hell is a forgiving spirit?"

"Well, somebody who *doesn't* have one is mean-spirited and wants you to grovel, keeping you in suspense and then saying, 'Hell no. You're not forgiven.' A person with a forgiving spirit says, 'We're all human. We all make mistakes. I forgive you.'"

"Do you have addresses for all three?"

"Arthur's homeless. He's going to be a challenge. We can start with the V.A."

"And Patrice?"

"I'm really hoping you have some solid advice for me."

"We shall see."

His cell phone rang with a 512 number. "Hello?"

"Hey, Charlie, where ya at?" Skinny even came through the

phone with force.

"Margo and I are in Houston, planning our approach."

"Well, guess who else is in Houston!"

"You?"

"Yep. And guess who's with me!"

"Lucy?"

"You're two for two! Where ya staying? Marriott? Getting points? We want to come over there and buy y'all a welcome-to-Texas drink."

"I grew up around here, remember?"

"Okay yours will be a welcome-*back*-to-Texas drink. How's everything working out between you two? You probably can't talk, right?"

"That's true. Hang on. I'll check with Margo."

Muffling the phone, he said, "The undertaker and his wife are in town and want to meet up for moral support."

"Tonight?"

"Want me to put them off till tomorrow?"

"I think you and I need one more night alone."

Charlie uncovered the mouthpiece. "Why don't you meet us at the Waffle House at 8 tomorrow?"

"We don't want to intrude. We just want to send you off with a good frame of mind."

"That's what we figured. We just want to have one more night alone. Know what I mean?"

"10-4! See you in the morning 8 sharp."

"Oh boy," Margo said. On the way back to their room, Charlie told he about Skinny and Lucy's bizarre phone sex game.

"It makes an odd sort of sense. The excitement without the cheating. Why didn't you think of that?"

Because I was stupid."

"I'm going to take a hot shower," she told him. "So I'll say goodnight now." They shared a prolonged hug. *I feel like I'm drowning and I'm clinging to her hard because I'm afraid to let go.*

She patted him on the back. "It'll be all right."

"I'm going to try to stay awake for you, but just in case, sweet dreams."

"Take your meds."

"Okay."

Chapter 35

Even though Margo had never met Skinny, she spotted him right away.

"Hey, Skinny. How's it hanging?" she asked.

He laughed. "Down and to the left1" He took a long up-and-down survey. "So, hubby told you about our little game. How did you know who I was?"

"I just looked for the biggest cowboy hat," she said.

"Honey, you're in Texas. *Everybody* has a big ol' cowboy hat."

Lucy shook her hand. "Hi, I'm Lucinda." She turned to Charlie. "I'm still waitin' for that dick pic, darlin'."

"Ease into it, mama. Don't scare away our new friends."

"When I was living in Houston, we didn't regard any city above Dallas as really Texan," said Charlie.

Skinny tapped his forehead. "The Lone Star attitude is in here."

"And in our hearts," added Lucy. "Right under this big left titty." She hefted it to demonstrate.

"Mama! Behave yourself! Sorry, y'all. She don't get out much."

"He keeps me chained to the bed."

"Y'all can imagine what would happen if I let her loose."

"So, to what do we owe the pleasure of your presence?" asked Charlie.

"Well, several reasons. I want to offer our assistance in any way possible and, frankly, I want to see how this turns out."

"Not much to see so far," offered Margo.

"We're going to Ralph's after breakfast. He's living in his mama's house in Sugarland."

"Just so you know, Lucinda and I are checking into the Marriott till all this is resolved," said Skinny.

"We are anxious to see how this will fit in the book."

"This shouldn't take long. We'll meet up with you guys for lunch," said Charlie.

"Slow and steady as she goes," said Margo.

"And if anybody gets shot, we're here to help bury the body."

"Not funny, sugar," said Lucy.

On the way back to the room, Charlie said, "You don't have to come with me. I can handle this one alone."

Margo grabbed his arm. "Please don't make me stay with these awful, but well-intentioned people."

"Okay. Ralph's going to like you anyway."

Twenty minutes later they pulled up in front of a brown tract home. The front yard, surrounded by a cyclone fence, was overcome with weeds.

Charlie announced their presence on the way to the front door.

"Ralphie, it's Charlie!"

The door flew open and a big, burly man threw his arms around Charlie.

"I knew you'd come!"

"What do you mean?"

"Randy called out of the blue a few months ago. He said you were tracking down people from the past to even the score. I wasn't sure what he meant so I bought me a 4-10 shotgun. You know former felons aren't supposed to own firearms, right?"

"Ralph, I'm here to even the score by apologizing for what you went through because of me."

"I'm wondering what you're doing in Texas," said Margo.

"Nice to meet you, sweetheart. You probably don't remember. I met you a long time ago."

"Uh no, Ralph, that was Connie."

"Oh yeah. She was Chinese."

"Korean, but that doesn't matter. Margo wants to know why, if you're one of my New York friends, you're living in Texas."

"Charlie boy and I always had that in common. Shitty times in Texas. When I went to New York to live with my dad, my mom stayed here in Sugarland. I moved back down here ten years ago when mom passed and the county was going to take the house."

"I'm here to apologize, Ralph. You did those three years in Fishkill because you were holding on to my 20 keys."

"It's not your fault; I was doing a favor for a friend. And it's definitely not your fault I got my eye poked out. It was just a nasty, scary place."

"Oh my God!" gasped Margo.

"Shit. Nobody told me."

"That's why I moved down here. Sandy said my glass eye creeped her out."

"Ralph, I am so sorry. This isn't right."

"Are you able to work, to make a living?" Margo asked.

"I got a settlement for my eye. And I collect disability."

"You know, Charlie, it's good to see you, pardon the pun. I really missed you. Tell me what you've been up to."

"Honey? Can you make a beer run? Oh, hell with it! Ralph, what are you drinking these days? Name it. Anything!"

"How about a 12-pack of Bud Light and… Charlie, will you and the missus do shots of Cuervo with me?"

"It's not even noon yet!"

"Count me out," said Margo.

"Honey, get the 12 pack and a large bottle of Cuervo Gold. Get the Reposado for our friend."

"Okay. I think I saw a liquor store as we were coming up the street."

"Thanks. I think we'll spark up this joint while we're waiting. What do you say, Ralph?"

"I don't know. They keep threatening to drug test us at the VA as a requirement for our disability checks."

"Tell you what, why don't you just stash it somewhere and burn it when you're sure it's okay?"

"I'd like that, but this is Texas and I don't want to go back to prison. You'd better keep it."

Charlie looked up at his wife standing in the doorway. She looked like she could cry at any moment. "Hurry back, hon."

He turned to Ralph with a smile pasted on. "Let's see. What have I been up to? Before we get into that, can I use your bathroom?"

"Down the hall, second door on the left."

The first door on the left was Ralph's bedroom. There were a couple plates and a full ash tray by a mattress on the floor. The bathroom floor bowed a little and a ragged towel was draped over the shower curtain rod. There was a Costco-sized tub of Tylenol on the bathroom counter. The bathroom, as well as the rest of the place, was rundown but semi-clean.

"Okay," said Charlie. "I noticed you shop at Costco. Smart man."

"Yeah. The headaches get real bad sometimes and I go through a lot of pills."

This is fucking with my head. Everywhere I turn, the room screams, "Guilty! Guilty!"

"Sorry to hear that, Ralph. Have you ever been to Thailand?" Charlie gave him the highlights of his trip, making all the details brighter, sexier, and more exotic. Twenty minutes had gone by with no trace of Margo.

She showed up twenty minutes later, carrying three sacks. "I picked up a few things for lunch. You haven't eaten yet, have you, Ralph?"

"Just coffee so far today."

"Are Italian subs okay?"

"Great! If it's not too much trouble."

"I think you guys will thank me once you start drinking."

"Let me find us some paper plates. Let's move to the kitchen so

I can put the beer in the fridge."

"No reason we can't have a beer while we're waiting!" Charlie popped a beer can open and handed it to Ralph.

"Here's to friends. Gone but not forgotten," toasted Charlie.

"Out of sight. Out of mind." Margo grumbled under her breath.

She handed them sandwiches and chips on paper plates. "Another beer, boys?"

She ate her own sandwich much slower and watched the two of them interact. Ralph seemed to look up to Charlie and she guessed that it had always been that way.

"How about that shot?" Ralph asked.

"How about I play bartender?" Margo said. From one of the bags she pulled the tequila, lime slices, salt, and little white plastic shot glasses that said, "Sugarland, TX." She set it all beyond reach of the men.

"Reposado is a more refined tequila," She played the instructive bartender, informed by memories from an earlier life. "You don't do shots. You sip it."

"On your mark, get set, go!" Ralph yelled and tossed it back. Charlie shrugged and followed suit.

Margo pulled out another shot glass. "I'll join you guys for just one shot."

They clinked glasses and tossed them back.

"One more!" Margo cried.

She turned around and handed each of them a full glass. Again, they tossed them back.

"Uno mas!" she announced another round. "Anybody need a beer?"

Charlie was surprised to find he didn't feel that drunk. Ralph was very drunk, judging by the way he was swaying back and forth. He looked at Margo and she winked. *She's faking our shots.* His future father-in-law had pulled the same thing on him when they first met, pumping him for information about her friends.

A few minutes later, it was apparent Ralph should call it a day. The bed was covered by books so they put him on the recliner in his living room and covered him with a blanket. Margo put an envelope on the coffee table, propped up so he would see it right away.

They closed the door and Charlie opened the driver's door for her. "That was... I don't know what that was," she said. "How do you correct the path of a life that changed so much because you sent it spinning out of control?"

"Hey! True, I asked him to hold the 20 kilos, but *he* dropped the bag at the pump!"

"Getting him arrested, putting him in a place where he would get his eye gouged..."

"Jesus! You make it sound like this was destiny or karma. But it also sounds like you think it was my fault!"

"Buddhists call it cause and effect. Christians call it reap what you sew. You were the cause to Ralph's effect."

"No, dropping the pot on the ground in front of a cop was the cause and I wasn't present for that one. And I wasn't there when his eye was cut out. So, do you think I'm guilty?"

"I don't know. If karma works right, then that will be *your* effect!"

"Actually, what can I do for his situation?"

"Nothing. Check in on him now and then."

"What was in the envelope?"

"Just a little something for a rainy day."

"*I'm* the one trying to make sure I get into heaven. Let me make the grand gestures!"

"Even in the face of what happened to Ralph, you want to come at this just thinking of yourself?"

"Some people are beyond help, especially when so much time has passed. What could I, we, possibly do to make up for what happened to Ralph?"

"That's just it; we can't. You didn't need his forgiveness because he never saw you as the reason for what happened to him. In one sense, you can feel relieved about that. In another sense, you do something for a dear fellow human being that you once called friend."

"How much was the check?" Charlie asked.

"Why does that matter?"

"I'd say that amount reflects his value as a friend."

"His *value?*" Margo was on the outskirts of anger.

"How much *we* value him as a friend."

She was going to explode, but the new Margo decided to look behind his comment and figure out what Charlie was really saying.

"Look, if you and Ralph were drowning and I only had time to save one of you, how would I decide who to save?"

"Go on."

"It would be you because your value to me is immeasurable. How do I quantify that and put a dollar amount on it? It's a gut thing."

"That's brutal, but I understand it now. You would put a value on everything and act accordingly."

"That's how you make split-second decisions. It's all relative."

Margo was still processing their conversation when Skinny called. Charlie put it on speaker.

"How did it go?"

"Better and worse than I thought it would," Charlie admitted. "I have a lot to atone for."

Margo looked at Charlie thunderstruck. Hadn't he absolved himself of any guilt or responsibility just moments before?

"How so?" Skinny asked.

"Let's wait till we're together. We're still reviewing everything. There's a lot to unpack."

"Sure. We found a restaurant we want to treat y'all to tonight around six." He turned to talk to his wife. "No, dear. I said *six* not *sex.*" Then said to them, "Unless y'all need some alone time."

Margo and Charlie exchanged glances. "No. Dinner sounds nice," Margo said.

"All right then. See y'all at SIX!"

They rang off. Margo asked, "Where does Arthur live? I assume you want to save Patrice for last."

"Yeah. I figured my visit with her would be problematic and our issues convoluted. But Ralph's situation proved to be just as thorny." He faked a southern accent, "I said *thorny* not *horny!*"

She chuckled.

"I don't know where he's living exactly. The VA said he's close by, but that's all they said. I could really use a laptop."

"How about mine?" she asked. "It's in my suitcase."

"We've got about three hours till we're meeting up with the crazies. I have a few ideas on finding him."

Twenty minutes before meal time, they had connected the phone number with the name and nothing else. "Worse $3.99 I ever spent."

"It may be easier to find Patrice," Morgan said.

Skinny answered the phone with, "Pappas Brothers Steakhouse. Want to ride over there with us?"

"Sure."

They had an older model Escalade. Lucy jumped in the backseat and motioned for Charlie to join her. Margo jostled Charlie out of the way and pointed to the front seat. "You boys probably want to talk."

Charlie brought them up to speed on the ride over.

"I don't think you owe Ralph anything. He may owe you for 20 kilos of reefer."

"Bullshit, Leroy," Charlie responded. "What happened to being your brother's keeper?"

"How'd he lose his eye?"

"We didn't ask. We figured it was a sore subject." There was silence for a second then the Rogers' laughed. Charlie was offended. "Sorry. That wasn't meant to be a joke."

"We're not laughing about your friend. It's just that sometimes certain subjects create all sorts of tension and something has to give," said Skinny.

"I think the best thing you can do is keep in touch with him, let him know somebody cares, put him on your Christmas card list." suggested Lucy.

"We're here," Skinny announced.

"Already?"

"If Leroy didn't weigh almost 400 pounds we coulda walked it."

"Just think how embarrassing it would be for ya'll to have to roll my fat ass back down the street to our hotel."

They parked and entered the lobby. While they waited for the elevator, Charlie saw that Skinny dabbed a handkerchief on the back of his neck. He had worked up a little sweat just getting there from the parking lot. Charlie focused on what his friend was saying.

"We tracked down your friend Arthur."

"How? We tried everything."

"We called him. Asked if you could come by," said Lucy.

"And that worked?"

"Not the first couple times," admitted Skinny. "He said he was done with you. I told him you was fixin' to go into the hospital to your deathbed. He didn't believe me. I said I worked for a funeral home and I wouldn't have a reason for deceiving him. He's expecting you tomorrow morning."

"Wow! Thanks. I figured after our last conversation he had written me off."

"Glad to help. I'm going for the bone-in Prime ribeye. How about you, mama?"

"You know me. I like having a big hunk of meat slidin' down my throat." She winked at Margo. "Know what I mean, sugar?"

"Are you always this lewd and crude, Lucinda?"

"Do you always have a stick up your ass, Margolis?"

"No. Just a little more class."

"Ladies…" Skinny ventured. He leaned over and whispered to his wife. She sat bolt upright.

"I apologize if I offended y'all. Like I said before, I don't get out much and back at home I'm quiet as a church mouse. Because I am one."

They ordered their meal and kept to small talk about Texas and Texans, Lubbock and the funeral business.

Over dessert, Lucy brought up Patrice.

"No phone number, no address. She's going to be tough to find," Charlie said.

"We could check adoption records just in case she wasn't lyin'," Lucy offered.

"How do we find her if there was no baby?" Chuckie growled.

"I figure if we discover there was no baby, you can, uh, abort the mission." Skinny said.

"No, baby." Lucy admonished him. She turned to Margo. "I'm sorry. Everything we're saying is coming out wrong."

"Unless you want to know if there was an abortion," Skinny offered.

"It sounds like you want to find her regardless," said Margo.

Charlie had his own conclusions. "If it will clear up the mystery by examining all the possibilities: birth, adoption, abortion, lie, I'm all for it."

"Sure you don't want to see her, see how she aged, see if she still looks good?" Margo teased.

"She's 60. How good could she look?"

"Oh, now you've gone and stepped in it," commented Lucy.

"You, of course, are the exception!" Charlie said.

"You're an ass!"

"Yes I am. I prove it every day."

"If y'all want to walk back, go ahead and take off. This was my treat." Skinny turned to Margo. "Please don't push him in front of any cars. That's an undertaker's worst nightmare."

There was a breeze that pushed in from the coast, but did nothing to dispel the humidity.

"Your friends are insufferable."

"Agreed. But they're actually helping."

"Let's thank them for their service and send 'em back to Lubbock."

"I'll bet with this expensive dinner tonight, they think they bought tickets to the circus. Our circus."

"They probably want to stick around for the clowns at the end."

"They're also not used to all this glamour and excitement."

"I just realized something."

"What?" he asked.

"You haven't complained once today about pain. Look, we're even strolling back to the hotel."

"You're right!" *Now I'm going to worry that one little tweak will destroy me for the evening.*

"Want to go dancing?"

"You deserve someone you can *always* share a dance with, not some dead man walking or rather wincing down the street."

"Charlie, you will forever be my always."

"I'm not sure what that means, but I feel the same."

"Even if I'm almost 60?" she teased.

"Even if I can't foxtrot?"

"You will always be my cradle robber."

"You will always be my spring chicken."

One of Charlie's legs suddenly froze while the other one kept moving, pitching him into the street. A Mercedes swerved and barely missed him.

"Charlie, can you get up?"

He tried, but it was like he was on shifting sand. His legs were splayed before him, one in the gutter, one lying dangerously in the path of oncoming cars. *Somebody's going to run over that.* It didn't feel like the errant foot belonged to him.

A car stopped after almost running over his foot. Two young men in camouflage lifted him up and deposited him on the side of the road well out of harm's way.

"Are you okay, sir?"

"I've felt better."

"Do you want us to call you an ambulance?"

"Do I look like an ambulance?" he barked at them.

They laughed nervously. "Yes, please," said Margo. When they hesitated, she said, "He's not joking. I think something serious is happening."

Within a few minutes they were flying down the street to the nearest hospital.

And I was doing so well.

He was still conscious when they wheeled him in, but staff still directed all the questions about insurance and his present condition to Margo. The accepting nurse then turned to him, "How are you feeling?" and pointed to a chart of faces. "What's your pain level?"

John called. Even he preferred to speak with Margo. "He wanted to know if he should fly out here," reported Margo.

"Fuck no. All we need is more drama."

Lucy showed up at his room the following afternoon. "We wondered what happened. We decided that the ball you set in motion needed to keep rolling along and that meant bringing Arthur to you. Remember, you're on your deathbed."

"That's not going to take much acting," Charlie groaned. "Every muscle aches."

Lucy phoned Skinny downstairs. "We're prepped. Bring him in."

"How ya doin', old man?" Arthur was in a motorized wheelchair.

"I have to quit falling down. Doctor's orders," Charlie replied.

Arthur's demeanor didn't change. "You know, I really want to come over there and slap your face. It was bad enough you treated me like shit when we were kids, but just a couple months ago you slammed my Lord and Savior. I can't have none of that."

"How are *you* doin'?"

"Shitty. I shouldn't even be here. If I catch a staph infection or MRSA, I'm a dead man." He seemed to notice Margo for the first time. "Do us all a favor. Take this asshole out of his misery with a pillow over his face."

"Arthur, this is Margo, my wife."

He looked her in the eye. "Then you know what I'm talking about. "

"God, do I ever." Charlie frowned at her.

"Before you and my loving wife snuff out my miserable life, let me try to apologize one more time."

"The man you see before you is not the little bastard you knew in elementary school," Margo said. "He's not so evil anymore."

"The devil comes in many guises."

"Don't get me wrong; he's still got his head up his ass on a lot of things, but he's trying real hard to be a better man."

"It's true, Arthur." Charlie suddenly realized Lucy and Skinny were still in the room.

"My friend Arthur was messed up in the Iraqi War."

"Thank you for your service. Was it Desert Storm or…?"

"Yes, sir."

"How do you know this guy?" asked Skinny.

"The schools had just opened for black kids. Charlie and I hit it off and our folks didn't seem to mind us hanging out together. Other white kids just looked at us or didn't look at us because we weren't really there. They realized the only way they could really isolate me was to get rid of my only white friend. It was easier than they thought it would be."

"It wasn't about being popular or anything racist," explained Charlie. "Not for me, anyway. It was about Stephanie Anderson. She was the popular one. So damn pretty. She had a certain circle of friends…"

"The popular white kids. You know, the ones that become captain of the football team, cheerleaders, Homecoming King and Queen and ended up owning the car dealership in town or running the bank."

He grabbed Arthur's hand. "Tell me what I can do for you. I need to make this up to you somehow."

"So you can buy your way into Heaven?"

"No. I just want to try – and I'll fall far short, I know – I want to try to make it up to you somehow."

"I told you before, you're forgiven by a higher power than me."

"Arthur, Lucinda and I were discussing how we can help you and help my friend find salvation. We think we have a solution," Skinny interrupted.

"I'm listening."

"We run a funeral parlor up in Lubbock and we'd like to offer you our deluxe package. Charlie will be paying for the lot and we'll pick up the casket and services. But we can only make the offer good in Lubbock."

"Wait. I…" Charlie began.

"I think it's a great idea," said Margo. "This is a very generous way to honor your friend, Charlie, and to honor a war vet who gave so much."

"I hear cremation is the way to go these days," offered Charlie.

"Don't let him fool ya, Arthur. Charlie ordered the deluxe package, too," said Skinny.

"I don't know what to say. It is very generous and I've never been to Lubbock."

"I know this can never make up for the way you were treated growing up. Or what happened to you in Iraq, but when you go, you'll go with dignity."

"Arthur, it doesn't feel like we've done enough, like *I've* done enough."

"Charlie, I've got a gift for you. I sent away to become an ordained minister so I could help folks over that last little hump to Heaven. I never thought I'd be talking to you again, but now I can do something. Can we all bow our heads?"

Charlie was the only one who didn't close his eyes.

"Heavenly Father, I'm coming to you on behalf of this wretched sinner, my friend Charlie. He has been searchin' for you, Lord. I ask that you guide him home and take him into your bosom that he may find true peace and dwell in your House forever and ever. Amen."

All of them responded, "Amen."

"Now, if y'all will clear out for a few minutes, Charlie and I have some talking to do."

The others filed out. "Now what?" Charlie asked.

"I know you're still an asshole and you have to live – and die – with that. But I have moved beyond my petty grievances with you and the rest of American society. My time's drawing closer, probably closer than yours."

"Didn't they tell you I'm on my deathbed?"

"You're coming on a little too strong for a dying man. I've seen men die. You're not there yet."

Arthur gave Charlie one last long look and slowly smiled.

"Have a good rest of your life, Charlie. I hope to see you in Heaven. Tell your friend I'll see him in Lubbock."

Chapter 36

The hospital kept Charlie for overnight observation, but all he had were a few cuts and bruises. He was released the next afternoon and was greeted by Margo, Lucy, and Skinny. He handed Charlie a beautiful black cane. "This is just until you've got your land legs." He unscrewed the top to show it was hollow. "This is your handy flask."

"That kinda negates the safety of using the cane, doesn't it?"

Skinny looked chastised.

"Just kidding. But I'm only going to use it when I'm thirsty."

"Fair enough. You look a mite parched right now."

"I can wait a little while."

Skinny showed him a fifth of Jack Daniels. "You don't have to wait."

"Oh yes he does," said the attendant nurse. "Once we get him to the curb, he's all yours. Do with him what you will."

She turned to Charlie. "Ready to go, sir?"

"Please don't call me that. You're not that much younger than me."

"Sorry, Charlie. That's just my southern upbringing showin'."

They hoisted him into the front passenger seat in Skinny's car. His limbs had grown stiffer and he required a little goose from Lucy before he made it into the cab.

"Charlie, I need to say this in front of your friends, someone to bear witness when I say I've always loved you, but you have finally opened your eyes to the world around you and it has made you a better man," said Margo.

"Thanks. Shouldn't this go in your eulogy?"

"I promise you in front of these lovely people that I'm never putting you in a home."

"Thanks? Hey, where is this headed?"

"If you keep falling, we have to consider getting you a wheelchair soon."

"Ah! Then from there it's a hop, skip, and a jump to… Well, no. There will be no hopping, skipping, or jumping to the finish line. That's not how I roll!"

Margo pounded the back of his seat. "Always with the jokes. In funerals, hospitals, it doesn't matter! Can't you be serious?"

"Margo, honey," Lucy explained. "That's how he deals with the fear. Death is betting all your chips in one final game and, no matter what, you lose everything."

"He makes everyone around him laugh at every party we ever attended, crying babies at the checkout stand, nurses at his bedside when he had pneumonia. He'll probably die wearing a red clown nose."

"Asians giggle when they're nervous. It could be worse," said Charlie.

"I think Lucy and I are done in. We'll be leaving in a couple days. Thank you for letting us meet up with you and tag along. It's a shame we haven't been able to track down Patrice."

"Thank you for what you did to restore Arthur's dignity. And thank you, Skinny, for sleeping with my husband and you, Lucy, for *not* sleeping with him."

"It's okay," said Lucy. "I can spot the boring ones a mile away." She winked.

"Are you up to hobbling into a restaurant, Charlie?" Skinny asked.

"Feel like carrying me?"

"I guess that would be a 'no.' Let's do all-you-can eat room service."

The next morning Charlie found some of his energy had returned. They met the Rogers for breakfast near the hospital to say goodbye.

"Please stay in touch," said Lucy.

"Yeah, we really want the first-look at your final chapter. Does our hero find the girl? Stay tuned!"

"You do realize we may never know what happened," said Margo.

"Let's give it a month. Otherwise, Skinny, you called it. An honest-to-God cliffhanger."

"Nothin' wrong with that."

"I don't know. I would feel cheated somehow," said Lucy.

A male nurse walked in. "Or a nurse in the hospital could walk in and introduce himself as your long lost son."

"Too coincidental. Who would believe it?" Charlie asked.

"That's definitely not a real-life scenario. In real life that issue would never be answered, all your characters would die. The End. Or something would happen in the far-off future when all hope has been lost."

"Do you really believe the second scenario is plausible?"

"Who knows?" Skinny stuck out a hammy hand to Charlie. "It's been a pleasure." Margo gave them both a hug. Charlie wrapped his arms around Lucy and grabbed her butt with both hands.

"Hey! That's my wife you're mishandling there!"

"It's about damn time!" laughed Lucy.

"Not a good move for a recovering sexaholic," said Margo. "Or my husband!"

Skinny packed their last suitcase, slammed the hatch and crawled up behind the wheel.

"Y'all come visit. You're family now."

And they were gone.

"So, do you want to stick around a little longer or head home?" Margo asked.

"What do you want to do?"

"No. This is your mission. It's up to you when it's over."

"Let's go home."

Chapter 37

"Am I hallucinating or is that my phone ringing?"

"Hang on. I'm only one person."

Margo almost didn't answer. She didn't recognize the phone number.

"Hello?"

"I'm trying to reach Charles Wise. Is this the right number?"

"Who is this?"

"Peppercorn Adoption Agency. Is Mr. Wise available?"

"One moment."

She held the phone to her chest. "Charlie, it's an adoption agency!"

"Tell 'em we don't need any."

"It's probably about Patrice!"

He seemed to perk up. His eyes gave away his feelings because thanks to Parkinson's his face just didn't work anymore. *I bet I'd be a helluva poker player with this face!*

"Put it on speaker." His voice didn't carry so well anymore, either.

"This is Charlie Wise."

"This is Dolores at Peppercorn Adoption Agency. We're responding to your request for information."

"About time."

"I'm sorry. Could you please speak up?"

"No, I can't."

"No, he can't. Parkinson's."

"Oh. Sorry. Just to let you know, we searched and searched. It was about 40 years ago, right?"

"Can you just cut to the chase?"

"Sorry," Margo apologized. "My husband's always anxious for good news. It is good news, isn't it?"

"We found a match. In the interest of privacy, we notify both parties to see if it's okay to share their information."

"A boy or a girl?" he whispered gruffly.

"Sorry?"

"He wants to know if it's his child and, if so, what is the gender?"

"At that time, if we didn't have a blood test, the birth mother's word was golden. By the way, we're talking about a boy."

"Is there any way we can get a DNA sample?" Charlie asked.

"Again, sorry. His patience wears a little thin these days. You're catching him on an off day."

"I understand. It would be good for the offspring to know your family medical history."

"A boy!" Charlie looked at Margo with tears in his eyes.

"When can we meet him?" she asked.

"That's entirely up to him. He has your information. Give him a couple days to reach out."

"Can I still teach him how to catch?"

"My husband's joking. We know he must be in his forties by now."

"Forty-two."

"And how to ride a bicycle!"

"Stop it, Charlie. You're making the lady nervous."

"Sorry. How's the weather?"

"Kinda hot and humid today."

"Thank you for calling and thanks for the information."

"Thank you."

"You have to stop that, Charlie. You freak people out."

"Sorry, honey. It's either my brain's vomiting up useless information or I had an information enema. Which sounds better?"

Margo saw he was late for his meds. *That explains a lot.*

In the last few months, since they returned to New York without any leads, it seemed something in Charlie had given up. He talked often to John and Tina, less often to his nephew, Scott. Skinny and Lucy were calling less and less, especially after she walked in on Charlie, dancing naked, listening to Lucy talk dirty.

Sometimes when they binged on a TV series his frozen frame made her wonder, "Is he gone?"

But then a deep racking gasp would erupt from his slack mouth and she would see his eyes dart about like he had just awakened.

She dreaded the days he couldn't wait any longer for a shower. John stopped by occasionally to help and when Scott was home from college, his dad sent him over.

"It's fucking surprising how fast I went downhill." She wondered if sometimes her dejection was obvious even to him.

A couple days after the call, the doorbell rang. They both were watching some stupid talk show that he would never have suffered through a few short months before. She absent-mindedly wiped the droll on his lips down his jawline.

A man in his forties stood at the door, cleanly dressed in jeans and an NYU sweatshirt.

"Hi. My name is Bill Rasch. I'm looking for Charlie Wise."

"Yes. I'm his wife Margo. Please come in." She took him into the living room.

"Charlie? Here is your son."

That got his attention. "Son?"

Rasch approached his wheelchair and offered his hand. "Hello, sir. I'm Bill, Patrice's son."

Charlie leaned back to get a better look. "You don't look anything like me."

"Do I look anything like her?"

"Couldn't say. It's been too long."

Bill backed away. "This is not what I expected."

"Sorry," said Margo. "He's having a bad day. On top of a bad week. Could end up being a bad month."

"Maybe I'll come back some other time."

"Where's your mom?" asked Charlie.

"She passed two years ago. Breast cancer."

"I thought you were adopted."

"I was. By the Rasches. I looked up mom when I turned 18."

"What about the Rasches? Do they have a problem with you reconciling with your past?"

"That's a whole separate life and until I decide who stays or goes, I'm keeping it that way."

"Did your mom, Patrice, ever mention me?"

"She used to call you 'that son of a bitch coward that left me.' But in the end she said you were just a stupid, scared kid."

"We both were. Hey, you wanna beer?"

Bill looked at Margo for approval.

"Two beers coming up," she said.

Bill was a long haul trucker from Altoona and came to visit every couple of weeks. Charlie's energy was picking up; he hardly fell asleep in the afternoon these days. Around Christmas, Bill brought along a woman, husky but muscular with a wary smile.

"This is Rhonda. I met her in church."

"What? You go to church?"

"He told us before. He's Lutheran."

"Can you put in a good word for me up there?" asked Charlie.

"I do every day."

"So, what do you do, Rhonda?"

"I'm a hospice nurse."

"Oh."

"I met her when mom was sick."

Charlie looked at Rhonda. "Can you lift 200 pounds?"

"When I have to."

"You're hired."

"I'm not looking for a job. I'm here as Bill's girlfriend."

"My mistake."

"Actually, I was going to wait until Christmas Eve to announce this, but she's starting to show."

"You're pregnant? That's wonderful!" Margo hugged them both.

"And we're getting married shortly before she's due," said Bill.

"She?"

They heard sobbing and turned to see Charlie was crying.

"First a son and now a granddaughter! I can't believe it!"

"Rhonda, can I ask for a hug?" She knelt beside his wheelchair and was surprised at the ferocity of his embrace. "Thank you!" he whispered.

Charlie shook Bill's hand. "Thank you, Bill, for giving me a miracle that a year ago I figured could never happen."

"Can you call me, son, dad?"

"When the time comes you can call me grandpa, son, but for now 'dad' works just fine."

"Have you picked out a name yet?" Margo asked.

"Patrice Michelle."

"Very nice. This calls for a toast. Except for Rhonda!"

"Can't I have some grape juice?"

"Margo, can you get me my cane?"

"Charlie, new meds. You could get dizzy, fall over, break a hip."

"I know, I know. Party pooper." He was cautious, but slow.

a held Margo back from rushing to her husband's aid as he champagne flutes from the cupboard to the table one by one.

at I lack in speed and grace, I make up for with precision."

ly lost his grip on a champagne glass and it shattered on

ill you let me take over?" Margo asked as Rhonda om and dustpan.

'l find the useless old man pouting in the bedroom."

him into the bedroom. "Dad, she's just trying to

er surrendering my..."

Bill watched as the older man struggled to remember his train of thought and failed.

"What did you surrender?" he prompted.

"Don't worry. I lost it. Oh! My dignity! I need to do stuff. I'm a guy, the family patriarch. She doesn't need to follow me with a dustpan and talk to me like a child."

"Wow! That's a three-dollar word, patriarch," Bill joked, trying to defuse the situation.

"Trying to derail my train again? I'm on to you! I've got a legitimate beef here and I demand action!"

"You deliberately make my life miserable!" Margo yelled as she stormed into the room. "Wipe your own fucking ass! Dress yourself! Why do I have to remind you to take your medicine?"

"You're right. I'm just taking up space now. I should step aside. My time here is done."

"Now you're just being melodramatic!"

Bill appeared nervous. "I think Rhonda and I will be leaving. I'm sorry if we caused…"

"Please don't go," Charlie pleaded. "I want to see my grandchild."

"She hasn't been born, yet."

"If you walk out that door now, I have a feeling you won't be back."

"I should have suggested this a long time ago," said Margo. "You need to research the disease, check out the symptoms, steel yourself against the occasional onslaught of dementia when he accuses you of robbing him blind with vicious, nasty names, the more rare hallucination when he's talking to somebody who's not there, the depression that makes him consider killing himself, or the times when he's lucid, charming, and so very apologetic."

"Jesus. I've seen a lot, but I've never had a PD patient," said Rhonda.

Charlie seemed engrossed with *Jeopardy*.

"It's one thing to read about it, another to experience it up close and personal," admitted Bill. "Are we making it worse for him?"

"What a sweet thing to ask! No. You guys shine some light into the shadows. And now that there's a baby in the picture…"

"Is Rhonda safe around him? Will our baby be safe?"

"I don't believe he would do anything to hurt the chance to see his grandchild. But he has his dark, bad days. The safe thing would be to call ahead."

"The sane and safe thing would be to not put her in harm's way in the first place. To leave and not come back," said Bill.

Margo looked alarmed. "Please don't do that to him! You've given him something to live for!"

"He's clearly getting worse! He might miss us at first, but pretty soon he wouldn't remember."

Rhonda grabbed Bill's face and stared into his eyes. "Bill, I love you for trying to protect me and this baby, but this is the essence of what family is about. Your father needs you now and we have to be there for him!"

"Like he was for me?"

Charlie had watched the back-and-forth intently. "I'm sorry," he said. "I fucked up."

"Dad, do you know what we're talking about?"

"A baby!" he answered with tears in his eyes.

"Close enough for me," Rhonda said and turned to Margo. "Can I help you with dinner?"

Charlie beamed at Rhonda throughout the meal. He wore a bib and spilled a lot.

"We'll have to get you and the baby matching bibs," said Bill.

"You have your father's sense of humor."

Bill turned to Charlie. "This is your fault."

"I'm sorry," he said. "I fucked up."

"See, Bill? That's another thing you should learn from your dad. Apologize first and ask questions later."

They all laughed, including Charlie.

After dinner Margo tried to talk them into staying the night.

"I've got a load first thing in the morning. We were going to come out later in the week, but we got so excited with the news…"

"We're glad you came," said Charlie with a smile on his lips.

"We'll see you in a few weeks."

Chapter 38

"Merry Christmas!" Margo greeted the call from Bill and Rhonda.

"Merry Christmas!" Charlie yelled from across the room.

"Hi, we wanted to wish you Merry Christmas and apologize we can't be there. Because I'm over 35, they're calling this an at-risk pregnancy. They want me sticking around home."

"We're sorry to hear that. But I understand. I was 34 when we... They take so many precautions now."

"I'm going to try to get Bill to stop by there next week, but he hovers like a mother hen."

"John and Tina are going to miss you, too."

"Maybe we can make it New Year's. I'm not going to stay locked up till March tenth!"

"That would be great! Skinny and that slut Lucinda will be here."

"Can't wait!"

"Tell Bill to call us when and if he's coming."

"Will do. Merry Christmas to you both."

"And to all three of you!"

She hung up and looked at Charlie.

"They're not ever coming back, are they?"

"Probably not."

"I'm sorry," he said. "I fucked up."

"I wish I had a dollar every time I heard that!"

On New Year's Eve the call came in on the tablet. Margo answered it.

"Where are the Rogers?" asked Rhonda, her eyes darting about.

"Skinny, that walking heart attack, had a heart attack. He needed a triple bypass. He was lucky he was already at the hospital at the time."

"How's Charlie?"

Margo turned the tablet toward Charlie and he waved. "Happy New Year!"

"We wanted to thank you for the tablet. It makes the phone calls almost seem like we're together."

"I wish we were."

"Well, we know you're busy. How's the pregnancy?"

"Did you get the ultrasound?"

"Yes, it's amazing how much of a little person she looks already."

They didn't make it for Valentine's Day either, but they sent a beautiful card signed, "The three of us." And they called. It was a bad day for Charlie. He deliberately peed his pants and blamed it on her. Unfortunately, Rhonda saw the whole drama play across the tablet screen.

"You want me to die. You're just waiting for it! That's why you take such shitty care of me!" He pulled down his wet pants, exposing an erection.

"Ah, yes," comment Margo. "Another of God's cruel jokes. He finally gets one and has forgotten what to do with it."

The weather outside in March was chilly, but Charlie felt it to the bone though Margo had piled on two blankets where he sat in his recliner. His lips quivered, part chill, part Parkinson's.

Margo was feeding him hot oatmeal. He could still feed himself, but he had a difficult time swallowing and if he got excited, he flailed his arms and she found herself scraping globs of oatmeal off the walls for weeks.

"I'm sorry I'm such an asshole."

"Not as much as you used to be," she replied.

The tablet buzzed with an incoming call. It was Bill.

"She's a couple days early, but the doctor wants to induce labor now. We're on our way to the hospital. We'll keep you guys posted."

"Okay. We…"

He was gone.

"…love you."

It was late evening before he called back. He held his crying daughter up to the screen.

"Here's your granddaughter. Patrice Michelle, meet Grandma and Grandpa Wise!"

"She doesn't look anything like me!" Charlie yelled.

"Right now she doesn't look like anybody, except maybe Yoda," said Bill.

"She's got Rhonda's nose," Margo offered.

"She's got my checkbook!" said Bill. "She just handed it over to the hospital!"

"How's mama?"

"I'm doing fine. I feel like I just ran a decathlon! How's everybody there?"

"Charlie's having a great day. Me too. We're so happy! We hope to see you and the baby soon!"

"As soon as she's road-worthy, we'll be up."

"I want to see the baby!" yelled Charlie.

"Give us a couple weeks," said Rhonda.

It was April and Margo was wondering if Charlie was going to make it to his birthday on the twenty-second. He was in and out of consciousness, having more bad days than good. His leg muscles constricted, especially first thing in the morning. Margo, more often than not, woke to cries of agony and tears. She massaged his calves when Charlie would let her. He sometimes thought she was creating the muscle spasms and screamed for her to get away, which meant the spasms lasted until they released their grip.

There had been a late snow and outside sounds were muffled so the knock wasn't obvious at first. It came again, louder. Then the doorbell.

"Coming!" Margo wasn't moving much better than Charlie. Her back hurt from constantly lifting him. She was emotionally drained from Charlie's rants and accusations.

She opened the door to Bill, Rhonda and what appeared to be a bundle of blankets.

"Come in, come in out of the cold. Charlie, look who's here!"

Charlie looked up from the TV. "Baby!"

The proud parents clustered around his recliner.

"Can he hold the baby?" asked the concerned father.

"He doesn't have much power left in his arms. You might have to help him."

Charlie looked down at the infant, awe and wonder written in his face.

"Hi, baby. I'm grandpa!"

She clutched his index finger for a moment and he melted. Tears streamed down his face. He looked up at Bill and Rhonda.

"You came back!"

"Sorry, dad. I had to look after the welfare of my wife and child first."

"He knows," said Margo.

"I know," confirmed Charlie.

"Are you staying for dinner?"

"I thought the diaper bag gave it away!"

"How many diapers do you have?" asked Charlie.

"About half a dozen. Why?" Rhonda asked.

"You'll need more if you're spending the night!"

"Not this time. I also don't want the baby to wake you in the middle of the night."

"And Charlie doesn't want to wake you and the baby either."

"Is he coughing at night?" Rhonda asked.

"Yes."

"I've been reading up on Parkinson's on my down time."

"Down time? With a newborn you have down time?"

"When she's sleeping or when Bill's pulling daddy duty. I read if PD patients are experiencing swallowing problems that can lead to pneumonia."

"I've had pneumonia before, maybe three or four times in my life."

"Do you have asthma?"

"Yep."

"Then that's your kryptonite, Charlie. If any of us gets a cold, we have to stay away."

"I'm not dying now. I have to watch her grow up."

"Then let's eat," said Bill.

A week later, Charlie's cough was keeping Margo awake at night.

"That's it. I'm taking you to the doctor in the morning."

Margo had a difficult time getting him in the cab. His whole body had stiffened considerably since the last time they had been out.

"We're admitting him now," Doc James told her. "We took some x-rays and it doesn't look good."

"Now?"

"Yes. And apparently not a moment too soon. You look exhausted."

"We're giving him some meds to fight the infection. We're going to send him home soon so I suggest you take advantage of this reprieve to rest up because you're getting to the point where you're not going to be able to help anybody."

He scribbled on his prescription pad, tore off the note, and handed it to her.

"This is an at-home care company in this area. See what they can do to help."

They agreed on a time when she should call in for an update. "It should take just a few days to knock down the infection and we'll send him home."

While Charlie was hospitalized, Margo usually fell asleep in front of the TV by nine, crawled into bed, and slept until 8 am.

"Hi! I'm Sharon. The agency sent me."

A tall black woman seemed to block out the sun at her doorstep.

"What time is it?"

"12:30."

"I must have dozed."

"No problem. I'm here to take some of the day-to-day care off your hands so you can have a life."

"My husband *is* my life."

Sharon put a caring hand on Margo's. "Let me help you."

"I would really like that. It's not cheap, though, is it?"

"About 45 hundred a month for a 40-hour week."

"Do it!" advised Rhonda when she called later that day. "Do it for your own sanity."

"I promised him I'd never put him in a home…"

"You're not. He's with you."

"Well, he will be tomorrow. They're releasing him."

"Take the care giver with you or have her meet you at the house to help you get him inside."

"Good idea. Come visit soon. Please?"

"We'll ride out on Bill's next delivery."

The next call was to John and Tina.

"Your brother's coming home Saturday."

"That's good to hear."

"I'm hiring a care giver."

"They're expensive. Have you looked at rehab centers?"

"Yes. I want him here with me."

"You know, Margo, we wouldn't consider you a bad wife if you put him in some kind of assisted care facility."

"Those wedding vows were about serious commitment. 'Through sickness and in health,' right?"

"You're a saint, my sister. Do you want us to help you pick him up at the hospital?"

"The care giver will be here to help get Charlie out of the car and into the house, but it would be really nice if you could come by and welcome him home."

"We'll be there."

"Thanks."

Sharon arrived while Margo was putting on some makeup.

"You're early."

"I like to see what I can do to prepare the house for his return. Would you like for me to go to the hospital with you?"

"No, you're good. I'll text you when we're getting close."

Dr. Brain met her at the hospital. "They had a tough time getting the mucus out of his lungs. When you lose the ability to speak with force, you have an equally difficult time coughing up all that junk."

"Could this happen again?"

"He has what we call recurrent pneumonia. If a patient has a history of pneumonia occurring more than two or three times during his life, more than likely he's going to get it again and someday it may kill him. In fact, they used to call it 'the old man's friend,' because it's a relatively rapid and painless way to die."

"I'd like to keep him around."

"Does he smoke? Do you smoke? I saw a history of asthma on his chart. Those are a couple of triggers, but really there are so many threats: viruses, fungus, parasites, bacteria that a compromised immune system remains embattled until it is finally overwhelmed."

The doctor saw the fear and depression that fought for prominence on Margo's face. She tried to soften the blow. "But what do I know? I'm not a pulmonologist, I'm a neurologist. Charlie is a resolute and determined individual. If bullheadedness determined our longevity, I would give him 50 more years."

"He was bullheaded and determined he was dying," Margo pointed out.

"If that's what he wants, we can't stop him."

Dr. Brain gave her an awkward hug and left. Margo walked into Charlie's room.

"As soon as I can get a nurse in here with a wheelchair, we're going home."

Charlie was silent, staring straight ahead as the taxi headed home.

"You should just drop me off at the next corner." Charlie's voice was just above a whisper.

"So, now you're hosting a pity party. We've been through worst. This is nothing."

"That shitty little hospital has paper-thin walls. Do you think I want to be a burden any longer? Damn, Margo, haven't I fucked up your life enough?"

"What about that little girl, Charlie? We have a family now, something we were denied a long time ago. Stick around and enjoy it with me! We earned this! Come on, aren't you excited to see what happens next?"

"Tell you what; I'll stick around till I get a better offer."

"Deal."

Sharon heard the cab pull up and ran to help Margo get Charlie from the car to the living room.

"Who the hell are you?" asked Charlie.

"This is Sharon. She's going to be helping me around the house."

"Just as long as she's not wiping my ass or jumping in the shower with me."

"She's not here for you, she's here for me."

"I thought you were going to get me a little Asian girl."

"I said…"

To Sharon he asked, "Can you lift 200 pounds?"

"I can bench-press 250."

"You're hired."

Margo's gratitude soon grew as Sharon's role in the household expanded. She showed up at 9 am every morning and stayed until dinner was cooked and on the table. And, contrary to what she had told Charlie, she bathed him and hoisted him onto and off the toilet seat. She convinced Margo to buy a bidet and the blast of water helped.

John and Tina loved her. They discovered she had a sweet tooth for red velvet cupcakes and brought her half a dozen every time they came to visit.

On one visit, John brought up the book.

"Whatever happened to it?" he asked Charlie.

"It's around here someplace."

Margo mouthed a silent sarcastic "thanks" at John who shrugged.

"I don't have time to look around right now," she told Charlie. "But we'll find it."

"I think I know where it is," offered Sharon. She came back from the bedroom with the dog-eared manuscript.

"My book!" Charlie exclaimed.

"Where was it?" Margo asked.

"Under the bed on Charlie's side. I was cleaning out the dust bunnies and there it was."

"Thank you for getting rid of the dust. Charlie could very easily get some type of respiratory infection."

"What are you going to do with the book?" John asked Margo.

"It really is quite good," said Tina. "You should do something with it."

"Thanks," said Charlie.

"What am I supposed to do with it? I don't know anyone in the publishing industry, do you?" asked Margo.

"No," said John sadly.

"I do," said Sharon. "My last patient was the wife of a famous publisher firm."

"What do you think, Charlie? Does the book have an ending?"

"Close enough."

"Do we know what happened to the thumb drive it was on?"

"I couldn't even tell you what it looks like."

"So, for all intents and purposes this ream of paper is the only copy in existence."

"We should scan it, print out another paper copy, and put it on another thumb drive."

"Can you guys stick around and keep Charlie company while Sharon and I take care of that and get a few things at the store?"

"Sure. Can you print two copies?"

"Sure," Margo replied.

They bundled up and left with the manuscript.

"Are you excited about maybe finally getting this thing published?" John asked his brother.

"I'll believe it when I see it. I think the book is cursed."

"I'm looking forward to seeing a real hardcover book with my father's name on the cover."

"That would be kinda cool," Tina commented.

John's phone rang. Caller ID said it was their son, Scott.

"Scott, is everything okay?" He noticed everyone was interested in the conversation so it put it on speaker.

"What are you doing with Scott's phone? Where's Scott?"

"This is Officer Madden of the highway patrol. There was an accident and he has been transported by ambulance to Stanford General."

Tina had turned pale. "Oh my god, oh my god, oh my god!"

"I'm on my way, Officer!" said John, already headed for the door. He suddenly remembered his promise to Margo and turned to Tina.

"Can you stay with Charlie? I'll let you know…"

"Hell no! He's my son, too! Charlie, you'll be all right till they get back, right?"

"Of course! Go! Go!"

"Did they say what happened?" Tina asked as they headed for the door.

"You heard the call. They didn't tell me shit!"

The door slammed behind them. "Bye!" Charlie whispered.

Where is that thumb drive? The suitcase! Now where was the suitcase? *Under the bed!*

He slowly made his way by wheelchair into the bedroom. *I hope*

Scott is all right.

He pulled himself out of the wheelchair and rolled onto the bed. From there, it was easy to slide down to the floor and onto his elbows.

It was dark under the bed, but he could make out the bulky shadow of the suitcase resting close to Margo's side of the bed. He caught the side of it with his fingertips and pulled it toward him. It felt empty, but a thumb drive weighed nothing.

The suitcase was covered with a thin layer of dust. Obviously Sharon had not cleaned Margo's side of the room yet.

There were two outside pockets, the most likely place for the thumb drive. He opened the little pocket at top, feeling around the lining of the pocket and felt something. He pulled it out. The leftover joint! He chuckled, remembering the confrontation in New Orleans with the first one. He had lost track of the second one and here it was!

He quickly gave up his search for the thumb drive. *If I'm going to smoke this, I'd better hurry.*

He had a straight shot to the backyard, but it was chilly and he knew he needed a jacket. He grabbed Margo's bathrobe, threw it around his shoulders and climbed up into his wheelchair.

He was excited to be doing something naughty again. Sure, pot was legal now, but he knew that Margo would not approve. He sat on the deck and looked at the neglected backyard. The neighbor kid had outgrown his landscaping business and they hadn't found anyone to replace him.

He saw an ashtray on the little table next to him: clean, no butts, but with a book of matches for anyone so inclined. *Shame! Margo was smoking again. Or maybe Sharon?*

A mystery for another day. He struck the first match which was promptly blown out by the breeze. It didn't help he was shaking from the chill and his body was jonesing for his meds.

He cupped the joint as the second match flared up. He managed to get it to the tip before it, too, was dispatched by the wind. There was a thin curl of smoke at the end of the joint and, sucking, he finally got a decent hit. He could feel the smoke as it snaked down into his lungs. It tickled the cilia, the tiny hairs that he had read sweep the lungs about 36 thousand times an hour. He coughed and wheezed a bit. *Just like the old days!*

He took one more hit as he heard car doors slam. He had to abandon the roach in the ashtray and roll back in before they caught him.

Sharon and Margo found him sitting at the dining room table as though he had never moved the whole time they were gone.

Margo looked around. "Where are John and Tina?'

"Scott was in some kind of accident. They had to go."

"They could have called." Her phone rang. It was them.

"Sorry we had to ditch Charlie," said John. "We're over here at Stanford General. Scott got t-boned by a cheerleader and it snapped his pelvis. They're doing a CT scan right now."

"Wow! Keep us posted. Don't worry about Charlie. He's still sitting..." Margo caught an old, familiar scent.

"Charlie, have you been smoking pot?"

"Maybe."

"You idiot! You just got out of the hospital with pneumonia. What were you thinking?"

"We'll hang up now," said John. "You've got your own situation to deal with."

Margo called the pulmonologist. "Just one or two puffs? That shouldn't be life-threatening, but his lungs can't handle anything like that right now. Keep an eye on him."

He coughed short and wheezy and faced down Margo's stern glare. "Just clearing my throat. Could I trouble you for a glass of water?"

"I'm tempted to pour it over your head!"

Sharon came up behind her and grabbed the glass. "I got it."

Rhonda and Patrice surprised them the following day. Rhonda placed the baby in a circular pillow she said was meant for nursing. "The baby stays stationary and the pillow's big enough to balance on grandpa's lap," said Rhonda.

She handed a package to Margo. "This is from Bill." In it there were matching bibs that said, "When's Dinner?' Bill looked up smiling as Margo and Rhonda took pictures.

Charlie started to cough; it was quiet but insistent.

Sharon and Margo exchanged concerned looks.

Rhonda snatched up the baby. "Is it contagious?"

"No," said Margo. "We almost caught him smoking pot yesterday."

"What? Do you know how much capacity you have left in your lungs, Charlie?"

She looked at Margo. "Is he doing his breathing exercises?"

"The doctor said not too much too soon."

"Charlie, you can't smoke, drink, or chase women anymore! You got that?"

"How about cussing and porn?"

"Just take it easy on the heavy breathing. You'll pass out."

She took Patrice into the bedroom to deal with a wet diaper.

Charlie looked toward the front door. "Hey, everybody! Arthur's here!"

"He was a friend of Charlie's," Margo whispered to Sharon. "He died two weeks ago. We haven't told Charlie."

Charlie carried on a conversation then seemed to think he and Arthur were sharing a joint.

Charlie breathed in deeply and triggered a wheezing coughing fit that didn't want to stop. It finally seemed to rumble to a halt.

"Should I call 9-1-1?" asked Sharon.

"No. I can't do it. If he goes in this time, I don't think he'll be coming back out. Help me. We'll get his inhaler and put him in bed sitting up. Then I'll call the doctor again."

After the call, Margo came into the bedroom where Sharon was playing chess with Charlie.

"He's sending oxygen tanks."

The oxygen arrived and between the delivery driver and Sharon, Margo felt ready to handle any oxygen contingency.

"Go home," Margo told Sharon. "We've had a long day. Tomorrow probably will be, too."

"Yeah. I'm here with her. Go ahead and take off," said Rhonda.

Sharon gave them both a hug and quietly left.

"You need to go, too. You've got the baby. I've got this."

"Okay, but I called Bill and he's on his way. He should be here in about an hour, hour-and-a-half."

"Great. I'll make us something to eat."

"He's picking up something. He said for you to relax."

"Haha. Take that sweet little baby home right now. Be careful."

Rhonda seemed hesitant. "Go ahead. We'll be alright."

Charlie had another bout of coughing.

"It sounds muffled."

"I don't think he's going to be able to cough anything up this time."

"Let's try turning him on his side."

"That's for vomiting."

"Couldn't hurt."

Charlie seemed to calm in his new position. "Now I'm going," said Rhonda. She leaned over and whispered in Charlie's ear, "Wait for Bill." With tears in her eyes, she rose. She hugged Margo tightly and her tears fell unheeded. She looked at Charlie, sending him an urgent silent message. "Wait!"

Chapter 39

Margo had to lean in close. Charlie's voice was a whisper.

"When we first met you used to gaze up at me with such adoration."

"Then you made fun of me and I stopped."

"I wasn't going to have you build up some image of me that I couldn't live up to. I wanted you to know I'm not perfect."

"You were then, *we* were then."

"Why did you stay with me all these years?" he croaked. "I've fucked up every life I touched."

"Not every." She sighed. *Such an ego!*

He wheezed, coughed and was suddenly quiet. She wondered if he had stolen away until his body seemed to remember to inhale once again.

He frowned. "I don't feel so hot." And he was gone.

Epilogue

The room was hushed as John made his way to the front and looked at the small group of mourners.

"I want to thank all of you who came here today to honor my brother Charlie. I know you may have mixed feelings about him, but ultimately, you're here because you realized he touched you in some way.

"Charlie went on a spiritual quest to find closure and some peace of mind and he looked everywhere: Thailand, Morocco, even Texas. He wrote it all down.

"Some of his supporters didn't make it here today: Skinny Rogers and Harvey Goldman, among others. Annabelle is here to show her respects on behalf of her brother Harvey and Lucy is here for herself as well as her husband Skinny. Thanks to Charlie we all know who they are.

"I'm not going to hog the mike. I know there are many here who want to share stories about Charlie and how he impacted their lives. Margo?"

She looked around the room and took a deep breath.

"Thank you all for being here, especially Brahim from Morocco and Boon from Thailand. You both played a significant part near the end. He would be happy you came and pissed that we paid for the airline tickets." Knowing laughter swept the room.

"Charlie would want you to know he was an asshole for most of his life. He screwed around behind my back and ran out on a scared 19-year-old girl who found herself pregnant and alone. You deserved a better biological father, Bill, but you had a great dad with Tim Rasche. I'm sorry you missed the last few seconds of Charlie's life.

That was so goddamn selfish of him.

"Many of you aren't aware of the great transformation that occurred in Charlie. On a mountainside in Morocco…" she had started crying. "In Morocco he discovered what had pushed us apart and, I think, felt emotion for the first time in a long time. He changed into a human being, not perfect, but somebody who recognized and claimed the pain he had spread over the years and the miles. And he tried to make it right. I think he did."

As she walked back to her seat, Bill and Rhonda cradling the baby in her arms, approached the podium.

"I'm Bill Rasche and Wise should maybe be appended on there somehow. Like Junior, but not. I only knew my father personally for about a year, but I think we gave him something he had always missed in his life: a son, a granddaughter, and yes, even a daughter-in-law. I'm glad I got to know him and only got a partial glimpse of the asshole he used to be. Just for the record, he was a scared 19-year-old, too, when he thought he might be a father. And ran. I forgive you, dad, and I think Patrice would have, too. Goodbye. Godspeed."

More kind words were spoken until anyone who had wanted to speak had done so. And though Charlie had only been just "Jew-ish," Margo went home to cover the mirrors and sit shiva.

Printed in the USA
CPSIA information can be obtained
at www.ICGtesting.com
LVHW091155271023
762201LV00004B/709